Louise

How are you going
to get the other two
from Boston?

Good luck with it.

All the best

Bryan Moon

May 88

Bryan Moon

THE WESTERN KINGDOM

Part Two of The Grapefruit Tree

The author would like to acknowledge the financial assistance given to him by the Banff Centre and the Ontario Arts Council.

ISBN 0 88750 703 4 (hardcover)
ISBN 0 88750 704 2 (softcover)

Cover art by Janet Moore
Book design by Michael Macklem

Printed in Canada

PUBLISHED IN CANADA BY OBERON PRESS

For Ethel Irene Moon

...Both sounds, my grandfather's laughter and the car exploding over the tracks, seem to ring out over the whole town. Down off Main Street, behind the hardware store, George Maclenan hears the booming sounds from the car and they provide a badly needed direction for his voice and thoughts. Slowly, drunkenly, his mind reels toward those sounds, searching for a place to light.

"Boom Boom. Boom Boom. What the hell, maybe they decided to blow it all up and start over. It's okay by me." He rakes his fingers through the dust beside him and encounters the cap from the bottle of beer he is drinking. Holding the cap carefully in his fingers, he raises it to his ear as if to listen to what it might have to say to him. Then he snaps his fingers and the cap whirls off spinning into the night. It snicks through the caragana hedge under which Bobby and I are lying. For a moment it seems he must be able to see us, but he does not. We have lain here before, invisible to him. Usually he is silent or talking business to someone who has stopped by to have a bottle of beer with him after work. Tonight he is speaking into the empty darkness so clearly that perhaps Bobby and I are back beneath the grapefruit tree across town and hearing him by some carrying quality in the cooling night air.

He holds the bottle up to the light to see how empty it is, and then he seems to address it. "Boom Boom. I've heard that sound before. No question about it. One and one half years of university. What the hell, it's more than most people get. One and one half years I heard that sound outside my window every night all night long. Making trains up and breaking them down. Boom. Boom. Eighteen years old and I figured I had it made. I was at university and by God I wasn't watching trains go by anymore. I was right next door to the trainyard where they made them up. Right where they started. Imagine that. Old lady Kowalski thought she had a dumb one. 'The trainyard makes a bit of noise at night Mr. Maclenan, but my boarders get used to it.' No doubt about it you old bitch. It made a bit of noise. It made one hell of a bit of noise. It made a noise like cannons. It made a noise like bass drums. It made a noise like a bowling alley in the next room. And you thought you were gulling the dumb country boy, didn't you? You dumb bitch, I loved it.

5

Hearing those boxcars boom together was...it was the noise at the centre of things. Yes. It was the noise at the centre of things. I would have paid to hear it, but I got it free in your boarding-house every night, you dumb old bitch.

"What was it Erdner said? Oh shit. Erdner. Things must be worse than I figured. What the hell. Come on Professor Erdner, let's hear what you have to say. You had some piece of bullshit for everything under the sun. Just lean back from that polished oak lectern and sling it at me. Right. I remember. The 'sound of commerce' line. Let me see, how did it go..? 'Go down to the trainyard some night gentlemen. You will hear the actual sound of supply and demand. Business is not an abstraction, gentlemen. You can see it, you can feel it, I would venture to say that you can even taste it. But down at the trainyard you will most certainly hear business being conducted in the thunder and roll of a boxcar.' Oh yes, Erdner, I remember all your good lines. Little Georgie in the fifth row with his ears wide open remembers all your good lines. So pitch it at me, Erdner. Just sling it right here, you crap artist."

From our vantage point, Mr. Maclenan is cut exactly in half by shadow. His right side is bathed in the bright fluorescent light that streams out of the open door of the stockroom. By contrast, his left side does not seem simply shadowed, but black. He is sitting on a small wooden keg. Beside him is another keg. He switches his bottle of beer to his left hand, and then with his right hand he reaches into his shirt pocket and takes out a small vial of pills. He thumbs off the cap and dumps three or four of the pills on the keg beside him. Carefully he picks one up and swallows it. For a moment we see his whole face in the light, slack and peering, as he looks for the cap to his pill vial. "You make me nervous Erdner. You always made me tense. But you're here now so you might as well sling a bit more shit. Go ahead. You might as well come out front and centre." *He gives up looking for the cap to the vial. Carefully he overturns the whole vial on the top of the keg so that all the pills are under it.* "We wouldn't want to come back tomorrow and find all the crows tranquillized, would we Erdner?" *It almost seems like he is going to giggle. Then he settles back.*

6

"Okay, Professor. Everything is set. You now have my undivided attention. Just lean back from that polished oak lectern and pitch it at us. Get out the old scoop shovel and make sure you got your gum boots on. No-one could ever shovel shit like you Erdner, so just lean right into it. But let me give you a little hint. I know a thing or two about shovels. You better use your back and you better use your thigh muscles and you better use your weight. Because if you don't your arms will give out in two hours and your back in three. I know, Erdner. I shovelled shit, the kind that stinks, and did every other backbreaker in this town and for 50 miles in every direction. I learned about shovels, and I didn't learn it from you. Nope. I don't recall you ever mentioning how my back was gonna feel after all day with a shovel. Nope. I don't recall you mentioning how even after you get that shovel shine on your hands you can still get blisters. You should have told me, Erdie. You said you were trying to get us all ready for a life of commerce. But you never mentioned how it's fifteen degrees hotter at the bottom of a six-foot deep trench than up at street level. Maybe you covered that the year after you flunked me out, you crap artist. Sure, I'll bet that's what you did. Shovels and pickaxes 500, Dr. Jacob Erdner, Instructor, a comprehensive study of how business really gets done unless you are a crap artist professor at a crap artist university." He reaches down to his shadowed side and picks up another bottle of beer. He takes the cap off carefully, and holding it in one hand and the bottle in the other, he drinks.

"What the hell, I guess a year and a half was better than nothing Erdner. Believe it or not, I made money out of it. When I underbid everyone on that sewer contract over in Belham they thought I could do it so cheap because I had learned something fancy up at the university. You should have seen their faces when I showed up on Main Street with that pick and shovel. The mayor and the councillors stood around and had themselves a little red-faced meeting. They tried to get out of the contract. Said I could never finish on time. What the hell did they think when they gave it to me anyways? Maybe they thought I was gonna stand there and read poetry until the hole dug itself out of pure delight. But that's not the way

7

it works Erdner. No sir, Professor Crap Artist J. Erdner. Bullshit can bury you. Sweet Jesus, you will get no argument about that. Bullshit can bury you. But you need a shovel, Erdner, you need a shovel to dig the goddamned hole." Carefully he raises the beer-bottle cap to his ear. "Here's to you Professor Erdner." He snaps his fingers and the cap spins across the light and into the darkness above our heads, perhaps clear across the town to where Jennifer is sitting on the verandah. Her voice takes up the story.

"So I just let people talk about whatever they like. It can't hurt you. It does not bother me anymore. I remember those drives. About halfway to the dance I would start to fidget, I guess. Robert would look over and smile and say, 'Roll it down Jenny, roll it down. If anyone can hear dance music from twenty miles away, you can.' And there were times I thought I could hear it, even twenty miles away. But that wasn't why I rolled the window down. I let him think I was listening for the music, but I could have told him what it was really for. He would have understood. It was a special thing. It was one of those things that don't wear out. It is as good now, remembering it, as it was back then." She pauses, almost as if she had learned the art of pausing from my grandfather, so that Bobby and I pause with her in suspense and attention. It seems as if the whole town is listening. My grandfather turns back from where he is leaning on the front fence.

"It was all the smell of leather, but when I rolled the window down, the whole beautiful dark night blew into that car. It was a smell. Lord, I was sixteen years old and on the way to a dance, and they never put that smell in any bottle of perfume and they never will. It couldn't have been anything but water and cat-tails standing in the ditch, dust from the gravel, maybe mustard, maybe clover, green wheat, ripe barley. It was different each time but every time it was the same. The sway of the car on those gravel roads and the night blowing by and the rushing sound of the wheels in the gravel and that unbelievable smell and it was like we were driving across the whole world and I was sixteen and it was all there for me. Though every time I swore I wouldn't, every time I had to lean my head out that window. I guess in a way I was hearing the

8

music.

"Of course by the time we got to the dance my hair was such a mess." Her voice has sharpened. "One of Robert's friends always used to say my hair looked like me and Robert had made a little 'unscheduled stop' on our way over. That is what he always said. 'Unscheduled stop.' Then they would all laugh in that way. I knew what they meant, but I didn't care. I still don't care." But her hands are up to her hair again without her knowing it, circling and touching and arranging like the moths that circle the yellow lantern above her head. "My mother used to say that the kind of people who said those sorts of things didn't have anything working above their necks except their mouths, so it didn't pay to listen to them. I guess enough people did listen though. When foolish people talk, there always seem to be foolish people to listen to them."

It seems impossible to distinguish between the foolish and the wise in the voices now rising all over Union. Voices rise with radio music from the rolled-down windows of cars. In reply, voices volley up out of the shadows beside the red glow of the Café sign. Voices murmur from the green dashboard glow of the cars parked along the bluff above the river. Voices stop and start with the match flare and the cigarette glow in the shadows beside the entrance to the hotel bar. People talk in the bright yellow light beneath the marquee at the Lux Theatre. Just to one side of the yard light at the school grounds Wayne Maclenan's voice confidently intones the name of each car that rolls by, its owner and the special ways it has been modified, while Patrick Stadler and Raymond Hueffer solemnly play the part of chorus, murmuring, "Jeez" and "No kidding." The cars themselves rattle, accelerate and brake at set intervals on the track they follow through and around town. As each of the vehicles now on the circuit rolls over the short incline that leads over the railroad track, their headlights sweep high across the central grain elevator illuminating one word painted in letters a foot and a half high: Union. The whole town seems to pitch and roll with sound and motion and light.

The rhythm is still hesitant, marked with silent moments when each of the storytellers stops to listen at the same time. Then puzzled

9

by the ensuing silence, each begins again, hears the other voices, and stops once more, like a person walking on a dark street who hears footsteps. Far over on the east side of Union, a steady blue light shines through the front window of Helen Stadler's house. Her voice comes out to where Bobby and I listen from behind the lilac bush in the front yard. She must be talking to her husband but we cannot hear his replies. "Try just a little to the right, dear... Yes. Yes that is good.... Won't it pull out further? Then try to get it up higher.... Yes, just there... That is very good. I think it is the best we will get tonight. When they put that booster up in Belham, they say we won't even have to bother with the rabbit ears. They say reception will be as clear as a bell. Now, be a dear and just turn it up a bit. You know I was just telling George Maclenan today that a forward-looking business man such as himself should get into the television business. When that booster is installed, everyone in Sortie County will buy one. Oh look, here is that contest I told you about this morning. Listen."

Out in the front yard Bobby and I strain to hear. We can just discern the voice of the announcer.

Brylcreem, a little dab'll do ya
Brylcreem, you'll look so debonair
Brylcreem, the gals will all pursue ya
They'll love to run their fingers through your hair.

"There it is folks, the famous Brylcreem jingle. Surveys show that even small children can sing along. But we don't want you to sing along, we want you to write new lyrics. Give us a brand new third line for the famous old jingle, and we will give you one of these terrific prizes!"

"I have decided to enter the contest, dear. A person who has studied Tennyson and Wordsworth should be able to come up with a simple line in an advertising jingle. After all, at least it rhymes."

From the front lawn, we can only see her head. Bathed in the blue light from the television, it seems to sit upon the window-sill like a flower vase or a bowling ball. I mention this resemblance to

Bobby, and we begin to giggle. We stop as she begins to sing. "Bryl-creem, a little dab'll do ya. Brylcreem, you'll look so debonair." In amazement we stop giggling. Despite the inane lyric and despite what we know about Helen Stadler, her voice is drifting out over the coolness of the well-trimmed lawn and through the thin scent of lilac with a choir-practice sweetness. "Brylcreem, you know we wouldn't fool ya. They'll love to run their fingers through your hair." The bounce has been taken out of the jingle, and it has almost become a lullabye. We creep back toward the street, confused and anxious because she does not sound as she should. The night has lent a frightening grace to everything.

On the other side of town, perhaps hearing an echo of Helen Stadler's voice, George Maclenan's wife is reminded of her daughter's nightly half-hour of dance practice. She looks out the window to where Tessa is sitting on the back porch. "Tessa, your father will be working quite late again tonight. You can speak to him in the morning. There's no telling when he will be home. Right now you better go down and do your practice." Tessa stands up and goes inside. Crouched low, Bobby and I run around to the side of the house. Bobby goes to the corner to keep a look-out, and I carefully crawl between the rose bushes and the house up to the basement win-dow. I lie there, stretched out beside the window, carefully arrang-ing the rose bushes so that the thorns do not prick me. Each small sting seems more painful because of the need for silence. The dirt is already cool and moist, but the concrete foundation of the house is still dusty and warm from the heat of the day. A light comes on in the basement. What I see there is at first incoherent. I am looking at a large open space, dominated by a wringer washing-machine, but on the far side of the basement is a room with an open door. It is the wall of this room that is the most visually confusing of all. It seems that the wall glows and that black bars have been painted down it at regular intervals. It looks like an enormous cage or the bars of a prison. Then Tessa's shadow appears on the other side of the wall, and it becomes clear that the wall is really a sheet that has been tacked up as a temporary expedient. The shadows of the two-by-four studding create the bars.

Tessa's shadow outline blurs as she walks over to the far wall and bends down, apparently putting a record on a record player. Then her outline sharpens again as she approaches the ribbed wall. For a moment she stands still, a profiled silhouette. In one motion her sweatshirt comes off over her head, and she steps out of her jeans with equal grace.

I am no longer looking at the silhouette of Tessa Maclenan, the daughter of George Maclenan. For a moment she is simply a woman. She has a woman's shape. Seeing her this way is, I know, somehow forbidden, even if she is only a shadowed outline. But I have no time to savour the feeling or to be intimidated by it, because the second transformation has begun. The second transformation is even more mysterious than the first: she is becoming a dancer.

She stands still for a moment, then slowly slumps over. Her head falls forward, her shoulders sag, and her breasts disappear from the outline. Her hips drop as she caves slightly at the knees. She seems to shrink. I remember the heat of the day and the tickle of sweat on my back. I remember the feeling of age in the late afternoon. But before I can grasp these sensations, she begins to straighten up. Vertebra by vertebra her back straightens again. The line from ankle to thigh is becoming taut again. The hips and pelvic bones shift forward. It cannot be taking long in time, but it is a metamorphosis from old to young and so the rose bush at my back may have grown up and away from me; I no longer feel the prick of the thorns. The vertebrae of the neck are the last to re-align. Her head comes up. Her shoulders straighten. Now she is the dancer.

She looks around slowly, as if seeing for the first time. And I must look around as well. My glance touches my hand. I am leaning on it and it is partly buried in the moist earth. With the fingers disappearing into the ground it looks like the trunk of a gnarled old tree where it spreads out in contact with the earth. I realize that like all the others in Union she is telling a story, and I turn back to the wall to see what else she will say.

She has discovered her arms. As her shoulders straighten up, her arms continue back until it seems she is finishing a race. Then, as if she has sensed my discovery of the earth beneath my hand, she bends

12

forward and looks down. Then, slowly, one leg begins to rise until from hip to thigh it is horizontal to the ground. Light appears beneath her pointed toe. It seems impossible to me that she can perform such an action until I realize that I am trying at the same time to raise the hand I am leaning on. She has made a discovery: upwards. Now she discovers downwards, placing her foot back on the ground. I must fight the impulse to look up past the eaves of the house and into the night sky. Twice more she takes delicate cat-in-the-snow steps. Then, with what can only be delight in the discovery of movement, she pirouettes; I close my eyes against the vertigo. She has discovered dance, and the story unfolds....

The Lonely Elk

According to one of my grandfather's dictums there are three requirements for telling a story. You need a place to tell it, someone to tell it to and a good reason to open your mouth in the first place. For the story I started to tell that summer, the place was at the foot of the grapefruit tree, and my audience was Bobby. Bobby loved to listen. He did not listen just with his ears; he used his entire body. He was something like a silent-movie actor. Suspense almost destroyed him. He would become rigid, his fists clenched, and he seemed to grow two or three inches simply because he straightened out with tension. Surprise was equally severe; his jaw would slacken and his hands would rise to either side of his face. Sorrow made him small, and laughter laid him back in the grass. It was only rarely that he ever said anything, so he never interrupted me.

I think it was the quality of his belief that made him such a fine audience. It was not that his belief was easily captured, although I was probably his first real friend, and he wanted very much to believe me. Instead, it was as if when he made the decision to believe, he did it wholeheartedly, holding nothing in reserve. The first few afternoons and evenings at the foot of the grapefruit tree, we simply talked. I did most of the talking, and Bobby did most of the listening. I was probably one of the first people to really talk to Bobby; he was one of the first to really listen to me. It was a mutually satisfactory arrangement.

I talked about everything, but probably mostly about myself. I told him about what I liked to do in the city, my minor setbacks and triumphs, what I liked and did not like. I suppose it was the usual series of topics for a twelve-year-old who has suddenly found himself in the position of being listened to. It was a good time. It was cool in the evening, the place was right and I had what was probably the best

audience I shall ever have. It was Wayne Maclenan who provided the final ingredient, the reason to begin the story of
the Lonely Elk.

It could not have been more than our third or fourth journey downtown when Wayne proffered the olive branch.
Grandfather was inside Mr. Barstow's shop exchanging a
last few remarks with him while Bobby and I loitered in
front of the store examining the horseshoes that had been
nailed over the door. I was questioning whether or not they
could actually bring good fortune when I heard my name
called from across the street. Wayne Maclenan and Patrick
Stadler were sitting on their bikes down in front of the Print
Shop. They were both wearing bathing-suits, and they both
had towels. Patrick had his wrapped around his head like a
turban, and Wayne's was wound around the wing handlebars of his bicycle.

"Hey, Jon-athan." They had taken to verbally hyphenat-
ing my name, undoubtedly implying that anything more
than a simple 'John' was worthy of scorn. "We were gonna
ask you to go swimming with us Jon-athan, but The
Wriggler can't swim."

I realized I was being given the opportunity to come back
into the fold. All I had to do was say something on the order
of, "Well who needs him," and everything would have been
fine. It was probably a temptation. Bobby was tactfully
looking away. Had I accepted their offer he would have
understood. Indeed, he probably would have tagged along,
and sitting on the bank, he would have been happy to have
the rest of us splash him and threaten him with drowning.
He would have accommodated all of us. But suddenly I was
tired of them. The thought of spending my time with them,
balancing, patching up and glossing over, looked like far
too much effort for a meagre return.

"No thanks. I guess I'll stay right here."

Their reply was final. It was Wayne who delivered the
message. "Yeah. Well the only thing Wormy is good for is

bait anyways. So if you want to tag along with him and a stupid old man, go right ahead. It's a free country."

"I guess that's why jerks like you are allowed outside."

That evening under the grapefruit tree I told Bobby about the campaign I had launched to change my name earlier in my career. I began with Mrs. Pender's devastating remark about hot houses, and it was a measure of my trust that I told him about it. Then I continued through my various attempts to change my nickname to Flash, and finally I told him of my triumph over Old Raisin Face. Bobby loved any story about the city, and with him listening so carefully and believing so completely I ended it with one small lie.

"So now, all over the neighbourhood they call me Flash instead of Hot House. It is way better, believe me. So you should change your name too. That way you get one up on all of them. It was almost like because I called myself Flash instead of Hot House that they started treating me differently. It's easy." I had almost convinced myself that I had been successful in changing my name to Flash, and Bobby was clearly convinced.

"So you should do the same thing Bobby. You let them call you all those names like Wriggler and Mr. Normal, and before you know it, that is who you are. Pick another name. Pick a better one, and we'll start to use it. You'll see what a difference it makes."

"Pick another? Just like that?"

"Sure. Change it to whatever you like."

"Anything?"

"Anything you like just as long as it is not something like Wriggler."

It was obvious that he very much wanted to oblige me. He began to fidget. "Don't just do it because I say so Bobby. Pick a name that you want." He raised his knees to his chest and thought very hard. I tried to help. "Just pick something that you do better than anybody else. It doesn't matter what. Anything that makes you special. Everybody has

17

something."

Suddenly he opened up and sat back. "My real name is Robert Baker Scott. Mum said that no-one could ever take your real name away. I guess that is something I've got which nobody else has." I stifled the reply that his real name was precisely what they had taken away.

"That is not what I mean. I mean something you know how to do or something you have. There must be something."

He thought a while longer, then he gave up. "I guess I don't have anything special Jonathan."

I leaned back against the trunk of the grapefruit tree and thought hard. If he did not have anything that was special, then I would have to give it to him. I thought of showing him the globe of roses in the front room, but even before that thought had completely formed itself, I knew what I was going to do. For a moment I looked at the twilight sky beyond the branches of the grapefruit tree. Then I spoke. "You have something special Bobby. I guarantee it."

"I do?"

"Sure. You are going to know something that nobody else in this town knows because I am going to tell you about it. It doesn't matter that I will know about it too because we are friends, and whenever anyone calls you a name you can remember that you know something that they don't." I paused. It was not a tactic. I paused because everything had become very solemn.

"I am going to show you the Lonely Elk."

"The Lonely Elk?"

"That's right, the Lonely Elk. And you have to promise never to tell anyone else about him. The only other person besides us who really knew about him was my Uncle John, and he was trampled by horses a long time ago so he can't talk. He is the one who painted the picture I am going to show you."

"I'll promise, Jonathan."

"C'mon."

We went into the house. I had no idea what I was going to say or do, but the moment seemed to take over, and in the bright light of the front hallway I simply played my part. "The picture is behind this door Bobby. Close your eyes."

He closed his eyes. I took him by the shoulder, and then I led him in front of the picture. I pulled the door behind us, shutting out the light.

"Keep your eyes closed. First you have to swear a solemn vow. Repeat after me." The words came to me of their own accord.

"I solemnly swear..."

"I solemnly swear..."

"To remain true to the Brotherhood..."

"To remain true to the Brotherhood..."

"Of the Keepers of the Lonely Elk."

"Of the Keepers of the Lonely Elk."

"Okay, you can look up."

The words and the picture did their work well. The Lonely Elk was as mysterious as ever. He stared across his twilight river toward the farther shore and the dark mountains and the glowing, blue twilight behind them with just the right amount of stillness. Indeed, now that he had become the focus of an entire Brotherhood, it was almost as if I was seeing him for the first time myself.

When we stepped back outside, it was as if the vow I had concocted had truly worked. The evening lights were being switched on all over town, and in the still twilight, Union seemed to glow with new meaning. We went down the stairs, across the front lawn, and sat down at the foot of the grapefruit tree. We said nothing.

My grandfather leaned out over the edge of the verandah and peered down at us. "Hatching plots, gentlemen?"

"Yessir, we sure are." I think all three of us were shocked by my ready reply. He disappeared from view; the Brotherhood of the Lonely Elk had scored its first triumph. It was true. We had hatched a plot. Grandfather's head appeared over the edge of the verandah once more, only this time he kept his eyes on the street and spoke out of the corner of his mouth.

"It looked like you fellows were onto something. Have you really decided on a caper?"

"We are thinking about it."

"Good. It's about time." He disappeared, and then re-appeared again almost immediately. "You fellows decide to do a job, then don't forget about me. I may be old, but I am quick on my feet." He peered to the left and right, and then added, "Whatever it is, you can count on me to keep my mouth shut. Mum's the word." His laugh rang out in the evening air, and a voice spoke from the street.

"My goodness, Mr. Caldwell, you startled me."

"Sorry Helen, just a few night plans is all. I can't say anything about it, though. I have been sworn to secrecy." He glanced down at us where we sat invisible in the shadow of the verandah.

"And how are you tonight, Ruby?"

"Ruby is not up here, Helen. There is no-one up here."

"Oh. But I thought...I mean to say..."

"It's okay Helen, I was just talking to myself. It is one of the afflictions of my age."

In the darkness past the edge of the verandah, Bobby and I grinned at each other.

The story of the Lonely Elk started that very night, and in the nights that followed, it grew. Bobby would ask a question, and the story would gain new substance in my response. He would express a doubt, and to allay it more facts would appear. Soon the story itself seemed to demand new episodes, and the Lonely Elk acquired a history and a goal, and The Keepers of the Lonely Elk acquired names, as did the forest in which all of the adventures took place. It seemed that I could mention no single facet of the Lonely

Elk's existence without having that fact bloom into further episodes.

The first few installments were simply the bare bones of what the story later became. The Lonely Elk lived in a hidden forest by the side of a rushing mountain river. It was called the Forest of the Western Kingdom, and it was forever deep in shadow. Only at special times of the day could one or two sunbeams penetrate all the way down to the forest floor, and except for those times the Lonely Elk lived in a pleasant green twilight. The forest floor was carpeted thickly with moss, and the Lonely Elk was more than happy to spend his days browsing upon it and his nights sleeping deeply upon it. Once every evening he came down to the river's edge to drink and stare at the farther shore.

Of course, even by the second episode, I realized that the Lonely Elk's utopia made for a potentially boring story, and so it came about that at widely spaced and irregular intervals the Lonely Elk would make his way, via a secret mountain pass that was known only to him, to a far and distant valley that was beautiful beyond belief. The far and distant valley was so secret that only a few mortals had ever heard of it, and even they knew of it only by stories, myths and legends that had been passed down over the years. Furthermore, of all those who had heard of the valley, only two were wise enough to believe in it enough to search for it. The discovery of this valley was the ever-present desire and goal of the two main characters in the story besides the Lonely Elk. I christened them Wolfsbane and Foxglove. The names were a great success with Bobby, and even now I find them highly satisfactory. I think I must have remembered them from some old Mark Trail comic strip.

In the beginning, Wolfsbane and Foxglove spent all of their time simply trying to track the Lonely Elk to the far and distant valley. Fortunately for the narrative, there were endless difficulties that came between them and their goal. It was not a question of them being inferior trackers. On the contrary, I assured Bobby, Wolfsbane was one of the fore-most experts in the world. Instead, it was Mother Nature, Acts of God and other similar forces that caused the difficulties. Time after time, just as Wolfsbane and Fox-glove were finally about to discover the secret pass, they would have to turn back from tracking the Lonely Elk because of such catastrophes as fire, flood, famine, and in one case, an earthquake. The Lonely Elk would continue on to his destination alone, and the two characters would have to wait patiently for him to make his next pilgrimage. Of course they could have chosen to ignore the various prob-lems that arose and continued to track the Lonely Elk, but by remaining to aid the forest creatures caught in the various catastrophes, they were, in fact, proving themselves worthy candidates for the valley.

Wolfsbane and Foxglove spent a number of years in this fashion. For Bobby and me, it took up six or seven episodes before I had worked through every possible natural catastro-phe. It became apparent to me that I would either have to find some other source of complication or let the two heroes go to their reward. I did not want this to happen.

It was not just that the story itself had become so impor-tant to us. There was also a kind of ritual surrounding it, and it gave us something to look forward to each evening. We would sit down beneath the grapefruit tree and listen to the town settle in for the night, and then I would launch into the next installment. And although some evenings the installment might be very brief, it always seemed that after wandering for a time in the deep moss of the forest of the Western Kingdom, some of its mystery would come back to the town with us. We would walk up the street, the side-walk still warm from the day, and then out onto the starry darkness of the bluff. There we would look down on the river and imagine that far upstream, in the untouched mountain valleys that my grandfather had talked about, was the fast flowing river where the Lonely Elk came to drink each evening.

The difficulty that I came up with to extend the story was predictable, but nonetheless effective. It happened that slightly to the east of the forest there was a village, and in it lived a full complement of dull and churlish villagers. I delighted in them, and lavished upon them all the care and detail that was at my command. Characters such as Mowgli, the Invisible Man and Dr. Frankenstein had to deal with a very poor class of villager, but I do not believe they were any worse than those who bedevilled Wolfsbane and Foxglove; my villagers were paragons of their kind. They always ate too much, and when in the forest they breathed noisily through their noses. They talked too loudly, and to the keen woodsmans' noses of Wolfsbane and Foxglove they smelled badly. They regularly made ther fires too large. "Pah," Wolfsbane would say as he and Foxglove observed them secretly, "they make fires that are all flame and smoke but offer no heat."

The villagers suffered from the most childlike superstitions, and they were also prey to a kind of mass-hysteria. On more than one occasion, whole groups of them turned and ran for their lives; Wolfsbane and Foxglove routed them from the forest merely by flitting wraith-like from tree to tree and allowing the villagers' belief in forest goblins to do the rest. The villagers never dressed for the possibility of inclement weather, and they were always poorly provisioned and unprepared for emergencies. More than once, Wolfsbane and Foxglove, on account of their great humanity, had to turn aside to help some inept villager who had become lost just as it seemed the secret of the far and distant valley was within their grasp. By means of various stratagems they would help the poor fool find his way back to the village and then listen in disbelief from the edge of the forest as the villager stood in the village square loudly boasting of his skill at avoiding the forest sprites who had pursued him. These boastful speeches were always crudely spoken and highly ungrammatical.

Two factors emerged that made the villagers formidable foes. The first factor was their sheer number. Wolfsbane and Foxglove had to exercise all of their cunning to pursue their goal when there were so many villagers to get in the way. The second factor was even more substantial: greed. For the longest time Wolfsbane and Foxglove could not understand why the villagers continued to traipse about the forest when they had such consistently bad experiences there. Bobby even mentioned this problem to me, but the answer was simple. One night, while the two heroes were lying just beyond the firelight of a villagers' campfire, they heard a strange and absurd story. The villagers had come that night to hunt the Lonely Elk, and the eldest among them told a story that explained why the villagers kept braving the horrid dangers of the forest. "The elk we seek," said the village storyteller, "is the most wondrous creature in the forest. He is no ordinary elk. His hooves are made of pure silver, and his antlers are made of purest gold. For the man who captures the elk, those antlers will serve as talismans that will grant wishes and all manner of abundance. They are known as the Antlers of Plenty."

Hearing this absurd tale, Wolfsbane and Foxglove had to stifle their laughter, but later on it saddened them to think the foolish villagers would never know what they knew: the true power of the Lonely Elk was as a guide to the far and distant valley. There, gold and silver were as common as clay.

And so what started out as a simple attempt to give Bobby something special of his own began to grow like Jack's three beans. The adventures of Wolfsbane and Foxglove in the Western Kingdom gave Bobby and me a feeling of sovereignty as we walked the streets of Union. No longer did the assured and secret destinations of Wayne and his friends bother us; we had our own secret destinations. No longer did the sense of purpose in those a few years older than us cause affront; we had our own purpose. We began to look out at the world with the free and easy gaze of the initiated.

At night we moved through Union with the same ease that Foxglove and Wolfsbane haunted the forest of the Western Kingdom. All along the east side of town was a road with a ditch that ran beside it that was overgrown with bushes and dried cat-tails. The path that snaked through the ditch was undoubtedly made by small animals, but it was suitable for Bobby and me to transverse the entire length of the town unseen. Like Wolfsbane and Foxglove staring into the village east of the forest, we would pause every once in a while to stare at the lights of Union.

The overgrown hedge that rambled down behind the hardware and post office, once penetrated, was more or less hollow, and it made a perfect route to move along and spy from. The narrow, boarded-up runways between buildings that once seemed unsavoury to me because of their ancient refuse, became for Wolfsbane and Foxglove ideal places from which to observe Main Street. The whole town was laced with such avenues, and we used them all.

One night while trying to extend our hidden pathways, Bobby had climbed over the fence that closed off the narrow runway between the Lux Theatre and the bakery. I waited for him to come back and tell me if he could see anything. Suddenly I heard his voice coming to me from above my head.

"Jonathan, Jonathan, it's all new."

I chinned myself on the fence, but I could not see him. "Where are you Bobby? I can't see you."

"Up here. I'm up here. Hurry. It's all new."

I had no idea where 'up here' meant, nor what was all new, but I began climbing up on the fence. I stood on the top of it and peered down into the runway. I was unsteady, and I put my hand out to the wall of the Lux Theatre to steady myself. I found myself holding on to what turned out to be the bottom rung of a ladder that was built right onto the wall of the theatre. Bobby kept whispering down to me that I should hurry and that it was all new. I realized what he meant when I stepped up on the roof of the Lux Theatre.

Bobby had discovered the perfect secret vantage point from which to view Union. The theatre was right on the junction of the two main thoroughfares of Union. Better still, no-one could see us because of the unused theatre marquee that had been built there. The marquee extended down the side that faced Main Street and the side that faced Centre Street. It was made of plywood nailed on two-by-four studding and frame, and it allowed us to walk around on the flat roof of the theatre without being visible from below. We were later to discover graffiti on the plywood that meant it had been used before, but there was also an almost rotted tennis ball which suggested that, just then anyways, the rooftop was our possession. Best of all, there were fist-sized holes along both sides of the marquee that had once housed the sockets for lightbulbs that had spelled out 'Lux Theatre.' They allowed us to see without being seen.

When Bobby had called down that it was all new, he had meant it. Standing there it seemed to us that the whole town was at our feet. We could see down the entire length of Main Street. It was just beginning to resolve itself into pools of light, the red glow of the Café and the warm yellows from the hotel and the pool hall. Up First Avenue we could see my grandparents' house and the Japanese lanterns glowing in the twilight. To the west, beyond the silhouettes of the grain elevators, was the darkness of the river valley, but at the farthest point west of us it seemed we could see the river faintly casting back the light still there in the sky. We could smell the river in the breeze. Above us the stars were coming out, and in the east the moon was rising so that we could see fields that lay beyond the town in that direction. It seemed we could smell the dark earth smell and the smell of the green crops. Just then we were truly Wolfsbane and Fox-

26

glove, spirits of the forest surveying the mysteries of the village. Bobby wheeled slowly around, his arms outspread, looking first at the town and then up at the stars.

"This is the best yet, isn't it Jonathan?"

"You said it. There's no doubt about it."

It was the best. I suppose I must have played the same games of pretend in my childhood that every other child plays, but the story of the Lonely Elk was different. It was either more adult or more purely childlike. I am not sure which. It was pretend, but it was not limited to clay, popsicle sticks and toy towns; we used as much of the world as we wished. We could take it with us down Main Street in the daylight, and we could take it up on the roof of the Lux at night. Then, at the beginning, we did not realize that the dangers might be equally substantial.

It was about the time that we discovered the rooftop of the Lux that the story really began to take flight. It was Wolfsbane who first began to emerge with a history and character all of his own. He had come to the Western Kingdom from far away, but he had heard of the Lonely Elk, and he had believed in him. He had devoted himself to learning all there was to learn about nature in order to prepare himself for the job of tracking the Elk to the far and distant valley, and through diligent study and remarkable austerities, he had become completely at one with nature. In every encounter with the villagers, he relied solely upon his knowledge of woodlore. Often, however, it appeared that he had supernatural abilities, especially to the superstitious villagers. It appeared that he could talk to animals and birds and trees, which, at first glance anyways, was certainly out of the realm of the ordinary. Bobby's belief in the story was very important to me however, so I never relied upon any sort of *deus ex machina* to allow Wolfsbane to triumph. Time after time I pointed out to Bobby that what the villagers thought was magic was simply the result of Wolfsbane's wisdom and accumulated nature lore.

27

The two heroes could be out walking in the forest, for example, and encounter a squirrel or a bear. After a momentary exchange of glances with the creature, Wolfsbane could discourse for up to half an hour about what the animal was up to, where he had been in the last few days, what he was intending to do in the near future and how he felt about life in general. More than once the creatures of the forest had informed him that the villagers were approaching rapidly or that they had laid a trap for the Lonely Elk at some point in the forest. But it was in no way a supernatural exchange that took place. Instead, it was simply a matter of Wolfsbane making a series of logical deductions based on the animal's appearance, the time of day, the season and so forth. All he was doing, I would explain to Bobby, was making the appropriate conclusions based on his keen observation and his intimate knowledge of nature.

It was because of this ability with the creatures of the forest that Wolfsbane gradually became known as the Master of Tongues. On one notable occasion he actually spoke to the mountains. It happened that the villagers once managed to catch a wild bear in one of the pits they had dug to capture the Lonely Elk. As a rule, Wolfsbane or Foxglove would spring the villagers' traps before they harmed any of the forest dwellers, but in this particular instance they were tracking the Lonely Elk over on the other side of the forest. Hearing of the bear's problem from a passing magpie, the two heroes once again had to turn aside from their quest. The bear had become hopelessly tangled in the net used to cover the pit, and in the process of untangling him, Wolfsbane himself became snarled.

Foxglove was in the middle of untangling his comrade when they both heard a shout of triumph from the head of the small valley in which the pit had been dug. It was a large group of villagers. The situation looked hopeless to Foxglove. He had just resolved to sell his life dearly in Wolfsbane's defence, when Wolfsbane himself told him to move further up the valley. Of course Foxglove refused, thinking that this was simply another example of Wolfsbane's humanity. They wasted a good deal of time arguing about the matter while the villagers came ever closer, working up their courage by jeering and shouting abusive things at the two heroes. Finally a compromise was reached, and Foxglove agreed to move a short distance up the valley and cover his ears as Wolfsbane had been requesting. Foxglove felt that all was lost, but he knew he was close enough to defend Wolfsbane at the last moment.

As soon as Foxglove moved away, Wolfsbane cried out in a loud voice, "O great mountains lend me your strength." Then summoning all of his powers of concentration he uttered three piercing sounds, "Ya Kee Ya." Nothing happened, and the villagers, who had paused in confusion, once more began jeering and advancing upon the two heroes. Once again Wolfsbane called out, "Ya Kee Ya" and this time the mountains seemed to rumble in reply. Finally, with the last of his strength, he called one more time, "Ya Kee Ya." On the third repetition, an avalanche sailed down from the mountain and neatly interposed itself between the villagers and the trap that held Wolfsbane. It was, I pointed out to Bobby, simply a matter of knowing the effects of sound on rock fractures and having an impressive enough vocal range to take advantage of it.

One of Wolfsbane's most amazing talents was his ability to move through the forest at a dead run on the blackest, most moonless night. Bobby let this feat go by twice, but when it appeared a third time he questioned it. Wolfsbane had rescued a hawk who had been wounded by a villager and had fallen onto one of the glacier fields in the high mountains. Because it had been necessary to travel for half a day across the glaring white ice to make the rescue, he had become snowblind. To make matters worse, the hawk informed him that the villagers had set a fiendish trap for the Lonely Elk right near the spot where he went to drink each evening. Completely blind though he was, Wolfsbane ran full tilt all the way through the forest to save the Lonely Elk. The villagers were as surprised and frustrated as usual. Bobby expressed his amazement as well.

"Aw Jonathan, how could he do that?" I could hear in his voice a real desire for a satisfactory explanation, but I could also hear that he required a legitimate one. I had my proofs and demonstrations all ready. I had been counting on an objection. Without saying anything, I stood up, went into the house and borrowed a tea towel. I carried it back outside, blindfolded Bobby, wheeled him about in circles, and then led him to the caragana hedge at the back of the yard.

"Where are you standing Bobby?"

"I can't see, Jonathan."

"I know you can't see, Bobby. But just think about it. Listen. Smell."

He paused. Even without trying I could hear the rustle of the hedge and smell the dry, chemical smell of it.

His blindfolded face turned toward me. He was smiling. "The caragana?"

"Right."

I took him to the pine tree at the side of the house and the lilac at the front. He identified both correctly. Back under the grapefruit tree I explained the obvious. Wolfsbane knew the individual smell and sound of each different kind of tree. In fact, because his observation was so keen, he could even discriminate between individual trees of the same kind simply by listening to the sound the wind made when it blew through them. After all, I explained, he was not known as the Master of Tongues for nothing.

It was a marvellous game. I learned the rules as I went along. We were rewarded for the care we took in our exploration of the Western Kingdom: though the heat had made Union dry and dusty, the Western Kingdom ripened Bobby and me. The forest gave us a place to grow that was all our own. Though others could only hope to get through the glare of each day, like Wolfsbane and Foxglove, Bobby and I were heading for the grapefruit tree each night, and beyond it, the far and distant valley. It made us Lords of Union, and although we must have known it would pass, as the water-melon smell of summer deepened, it seemed it never would.

The Sand Hills

While the Western Kingdom bloomed for Bobby and me, Union continued to dry up. The dusty, preserved spring-time was replaced by an equally dry and dusty summer. The heat was patient. Each morning when we rose it was waiting for us in the limp-curtain stillness just outside the front door, and it stayed until well after sundown. Still, there had been no out-and-out drought; there had been just enough rain to maintain everyone's suspense about the crops. The heat no longer pressed down upon the town; instead it hovered, day in and day out, in a range that was merely uncomfortable. Had it been slightly hotter, people would have relaxed and complained about the weather with a smug stoicism. As it was, if anyone opened with, "It sure is hot today," they could not be sure whether there would be neighbourly agreement or the irritable reply that the weather could be much hotter. The crops and the stands of trees around Union were changed from the usual solid blocks of colour into spindly collections of individual plants.

Most bothersome of all was that Union's weather seemed to be a purely local phenomenon. The Sortie River, for example, had shrunk back from its early summer high-water mark as it always did. The false channels that earlier had separated islands from the shore in the broader stretches of the river had dried up, leaving small pools of insect-alive water and numerous rock-to-rock pathways from the river-bank to the islands, but the water was not too much lower than normal for mid-July. The main channel continued to be as deep and smooth as ever because west of Union there had been the usual amount of rain. It was the same 50 miles to the north and south of town, and even in Belham, 25 miles to the east and supposedly much drier country, there had been adequate rainfall. But around Union the margin of cracked clay around the sloughs grew, and the cat-tails in the ditches were more grey than green.

The weather may have been a cause or it may have been a symptom, but the whole town was affected with an irritable dissatisfaction. It was Grandfather who came up with a project designed to revitalize everyone, and most of all, himself. His solution is probably still remembered by those who were there as the Sand Castle Project. He envisioned a sand processing plant on the edge of the Sand Hills, the gullies and blowouts north and east of Union. The plant would clean and bag the sand for shipment to any and all industries and manufacturers who used concrete or cement. It was Helen Stadler who christened it the Sand Castle Project, and the way that Grandfather conducted his campaign to receive municipal funding fully justified the title.

I was present when he stepped out the door the morning after the night he conceived it all. Even on that first morning there was a brashness and an antic edge to his behaviour that I had never seen before. Bobby and I were sitting on the verandah. We had known he was in the dining-room writing in his green ledgers, but Grandmother would not or could not tell us anything else except that we should not bother him.

Actually, to say he stepped out of the door that morning is incorrect. The first thing he did was crane his head out and peer at Bobby and me. "By gawd, it's here again." He ducked his head back in, and a moment later stepped all the way outside. "Good morning boys. Shows up about this time every day, doesn't it? Damn, it looks like a first-rate show. I have always said that it's the best time of the day. A wise man gets her roped down and ready to travel before noon." We were watching him warily. It was not that he was unsteady on his feet, but there was something in the way he half danced down the verandah that made us think we might be stepped on inadvertently.

"Good morning Robert Baker Scott. I am sorry I missed the vision of your lovely mother on a morning like this. I trust she was the grace of the day that she usually is. Never mind. I have come out here to give you two a little piece of advice. Call it a little something to tuck away in the backs of your minds to bring out when the need arises. I guess you could call it a tool for living. By gawd, that's not bad, is it? Tools for living. It kind of sounds like a section in the *Reader's Digest*.

"Tool Number One. How do you tell a good carpenter from a man with a hammer in his hand?" He leaned back against the railing and waited for a reply. When we made none, he started pacing. "Look at his hands? Take a look and see if his thumbs are a little mashed up by that hammer?" It was clear he wanted our participation. We shook our heads in unison, guessing correctly that the first choice would not be the right one.

"Okay. Some folks might say you should have a look at his toolbox. Take a look at his square and his level. If they look brand new then maybe you have got yourself a careless man. How about it?" It was not a bad choice. It seemed like the sort of thing he might suggest, but both Bobby and I decided on no. We shook our heads again, watching him carefully.

"Damn. I got a couple of sharp-shooters sitting on my verandah in the morning light. I guess I am just going to have to come out with it." He looked out at the street for a few moments and then back down at us. "Here it is, boys. A guaranteed, one hundred percent, over-proof product of

33

years of experience. I have built houses and I have sold tools and I have sold lumber. Gawddamn, I have even worked the lumber camps for a living. I have known men who couldn't build a chicken coop and I have known men who could build the pearly gates out of an old packing crate...." He paused. It was a long pause even by his standards, but as cynical as I was about his dramatics, I knew he had the two of us right where he wanted us. He was looking out at the street again. We looked out as well. The sun seemed to brighten with suspense, making the street look even more washed of colour than it usually did. He watched a car drive by and out of sight, and then he turned back to us. He actually put his finger to the side of his nose.

"Always look in his shirt pocket."

Bobby giggled nervously. It seemed that my grandfather was on the verge as well. He moved closer and spoke in a confidential tone of voice. "Yep. Take a peek in that breast pocket and see if he has one of those chewed down pencils that have seen a lot of words. That's the first sign. You see that pencil and you start looking for the second sign. Take a look at the back of his cigarette package." He paused, thinking. "Or take a look at the back of the envelope that he told his wife he would mail three days earlier. Or the back of the business card some salesman gave him." He straightened up. "Gentlemen, if the man has been figuring with that chewed down pencil on that piece of scrap paper then you know you have got yourself a carpenter. Yessir, it came to me this morning. If the man has been figuring it out in black and white, then you better shake his hand and tell him what you want done because you will be talking to the right man for the job."

He wheeled around and almost danced to the end of the verandah and then part way back again. Tapping his temple with his forefinger, he continued speaking. "There's no doubt about it. It all starts in the head. But it's when you lay her out in black and white that you start to see where she is

34

going to travel and where go lame. No question about it. A good carpenter, gentlemen, a carpenter you can count on, that carpenter is always figuring." He stepped over and slapped the side of the house. "How many words went into this show here? I helped build it, and I can tell you there were a damn sight more words than nails. Damn. It's just about all words. How do you order the material?"

We stared at him.

"Words, that's how. Now let me hear it."

We spoke in unison. "Words?"

"No doubt about it gentlemen. Now what do the plans depend on? Let's hear it good and loud this time."

"Words." It was as if we were participating in some sort of cheer.

"That is exactly right. You got the architect talking to the foreman, you got the foreman talking to the workmen, you got the workmen talking to each other. What does the whole damned show depend on. Sing it out and don't be shy."

"WORDS." We shouted it out, and Bobby rocked back and forth with laughter.

"I hear you boys, and you're right." He raised his hand for silence and pointed out across the street. "Boys, that is not a street out there." We stared out at the street. He spoke quietly. "Nope, that is not a street. It's more like a sentence that got out of hand." He went over to his chair and sat down, smiling and calmer than he had been since he had appeared.

"You figure these things out when you get up at the right time of day. Half an hour before sunrise, and by seven in the morning you have put in the best hours of the day. I have been figuring. Yep, I have been jotting down and I have been calculating and I have come up with a plan. I am going to go back inside and get my hat and then we are going down to Main Street and rattle a few cages." He stood up and walked down the verandah. Then he stopped by the

35

door. "Nope. We are not going to rattle cages. We are going to go down to Main Street and do a bit of editing."

That day on our journey down Main Street he used the same combination of bluster and sleight-of-hand that he always used, but there was something—I could not pin down exactly what, but something—that was askew. It gave me the same feeling that looking into one of the natural habitat dioramas at the museum always gave me. I remember the Coyote Diorama in particular. At first, looking into it was always like looking into the real world. I would stare through the picture window at the family of coyotes frolicking in front of their den. It was early spring in the display, and there were a few leafless trees and straggling bushes to one side. The whole scene merged into the painted background imperceptibly. After I had marvelled at the diorama for five minutes or so, visually convinced by the stuffed coyotes and the painted backdrop, a feeling of disappointment would begin to grow. Perhaps it was the cumulative effect of the *papier maché* den, the stiffness of the grass in the foreground or the perfect perspective of the backdrop, but the whole scene would begin to lose its illusion of reality. The coyotes' eyes would begin to hint of dusty, glass buttons.

It was the same with my grandfather. I started to sense a concealed impatience in the way he talked to people. Bobby sensed it as well. He began acting almost as he had acted on the very first day I had met him. He started looking at the ground, glancing up once in a while surreptitiously, as if gauging how he should act so as not to get in the way. I began to grow irritated. We did not stop at Mr. Barstow's on the way down to Main Street, so I knew we would stop on the way back, and I knew that whatever was troubling my grandfather would surface at Mr. Barstow's.

I was right. It surfaced immediately. Instead of sitting down and settling back in his chair, Grandfather stood up and began sauntering around the shop. First he walked over to the bench and began picking up tools, examining them

36

briefly, and then setting them back down. Then he moved to the far side of the shop where everything was stacked up and continued to poke around. After a few minutes of watching him pick up and put down various articles, Mr. Barstow spoke up.

"Rod, do you remember when Clarence Garner inherited all that money from his father-in-law and went away on that trip?"

Grandfather turned back to the open part of the shop. "Sure. He was away the whole winter of '51. What about it?"

"Then I guess you remember how he was when he got back that spring and stopped in at the hardware."

Grandfather paused. I think he heard something coming, but he was not sure what it was. "Sure I do. What of it?"

"Well Rod, let's just see how good your memory really is. Do you remember how he walked around the store that day?"

"By gawd, I do. He walked around like the God Woolworth come down from the clouds to check me out."

Mr. Barstow turned in his chair and began to speak to Bobby and me. "Old Clarence walked around the store, handling the merchandise and looking at price tags, generally turning his nose up at everything. I remember he had on some silly looking baseball cap from Disneyland or something, and he kept saying how he had seen retail outlets—he didn't say stores, he said retail outlets—down in the States that would cover a quarter section. Rod here took it for a while and then he finally said, 'Well Clarence, if you think you are going to find a substandard sticker by turning over every article in this store than I can tell you that you're headed for disappointment. You'd be better off just lifting that cap of yours, because what's underneath it is the only thing that is substandard in here right now.' Clarence got pretty strained looking, turned right on his heel and walked out without a word. It wasn't till later that day we found out that he had gone and bought himself a hairpiece while he had been down south."

"By gawd, that one travelled didn't it? He didn't show his face in town for nearly a month. Everyone figured I'd got off a good one. No-one believed that I had meant his brain. I didn't even know about the hairpiece." Suddenly he stopped talking and smiling. There was the start of comprehension in his face. "Just what brings that to mind, Blacksmith?"

"Rod, the way you've been strolling around here I wondered if you'd just inherited some money." Mr. Barstow's voice was very quiet.

Grandfather turned away and carefully placed the hubcap he had been holding back on its pile. He stood still for a moment, and then he turned and spoke. "Well, I guess there are a few things I wouldn't mind saying."

"I figured. You have been chewing on something for two weeks now. You might as well spit it out if you are not going to swallow it."

"Jerome, don't you get tired of all this?" He gestured around the shop, and for the first time the frustration that had been edging his voice was clearly present.

"All what?"

"All this. All this baggage. Twenty years of garbage that you have been piling up in this shop."

"Now just hold on a minute." There was a quick edge in Mr. Barstow's voice as well. "This isn't garbage. And it's not baggage. I'm not planning any trips."

"That's not the point. If it's not baggage and it's not garbage, then what the hell is it? Just what have you been collecting for the last twenty years Jerome? You figure your son wants it? You figure Henry is going to take it all? Or maybe you figure you can take it with you."

Mr. Barstow slowly began to straighten in his chair. "I don't know if Henry wants it or not. I don't even know what my son's name is doing in this conversation. The fact of the matter is I don't know what the hell you are talking about.

And furthermore I don't see as how you are much better off."

"I was not talking cash value, Jerome. You know me better than that."

"I am not talking cash value either. And you know me better than that. You're standing there slinging around the word garbage, but as far as I can tell you've got a house that's filled with the same junk. Maybe it's a bit better polished, but that's about all."

"Okay, but let's say a damn sight better polished, but that's not the point. You sit in here day in and day out and the piles of junk get bigger and bigger and where the hell does it get you. The whole damn town is on the same merry-go-round. Every damn place I look people are collecting piles of junk. Gawddamn, we are up to our asses in garbage. We've traded in life on piles of junk. You've given up. This town has given up. Even the gawddamned weather has given up. But I'll tell you this, I'm not going to."

Mr. Barstow had straightened as far as he could in his chair. I had never seen him sit straighter. "Just what in the hell are you doing that is so special Caldwell?" He never used my grandfather's last name in that way, and we all heard it. Before my grandfather answered, he pressed his index finger to a point between his eyes and began rubbing upwards. Then he started shaking his head.

"I've been thinking." He shook his head again. "I have had time to think the last little while. It's got to do with making something grow. I don't know. It's got to do with something that is going to be around after you've gone, something that'll last. After my brother died I thought I could get it on the farm. Then I thought I had it with the store. But where is that now? Where is this town going? It may not be much, but it's been the last half of my life. I just don't know. I have been writing it all down, trying to figure it out...."

"Oh Lord. I don't know what the hell you are talking about making grow, Rod, but you better take it easy. Just what is going on with you anyways? You say you wanted something that you didn't get with the hardware. Let's get it out in the open. You figured that George Maclenan was going to help you get whatever it is that you're trying to get hold of. But what the hell is George Maclenan up to now? Think about it. Just exactly what is he..." Grandfather was suddenly up from his chair and striding for the open door, calling back to Bobby and me to come with him. But before we could move Mr. Barstow was calling to him. There was no conciliation in his voice, but there was a kind of quiet directness. "Hold on a second. Maybe I am saying the wrong things. If I am, I'm sorry, but you are the one who brought up Henry, so I guess it cuts both ways. There are just a couple of things I want to understand, so just smooth your tailfeathers out and sit back down on them. I know what you are saying, Rod, or at least I think I do. It tells me why you put George Maclenan under your wing ten years ago. He was the one who was going to tend your garden, right? He was going to be the one to water whatever it is that you want to grow. Well that is all fine by me. But I want you to tell me something before you fire out of here. Why George Maclenan? I have never been able to figure that out. Why George Maclenan?"

Grandfather did not sit back down, but he stepped back inside from the doorway. He was shaking his head again. "He was a good listener, Jerome. He knew how to listen. That's all. He listened to me."

"Well you should have done some listening yourself. Ninety-five percent of the people in this county could have told you what kind of man he was. Just 30 years old and there was hardly a man in 50 miles of here who he hadn't screwed in the ear. Maybe you don't want to hear it, but in the last ten years he has got better at it. Good Lord, Rod, the only thing George Maclenan ever wanted to grow was his bank account. And there you were, saving up your best lines for whenever he came through the door of the store.

Don't think I didn't see it. But I couldn't figure it out. Not then and not now."

"That is too easy Jerome. That is too damned easy by half and you know it. It's not the money he wants and it never was. Maclenan wanted the same damn thing that brought you and me and a thousand others out here 50 years ago. He wanted the same damned thing that brought me in to build that hardware, the same damn thing that keeps me rattling my bones up and down Main Street today. Gawddamn. You think it was money that made me get into that store? If you do then you are a fool. All I ever wanted was..." He took a step forward as if doing so would help him find the right words. "I don't know. It wasn't the money. I wanted to be at the centre, Jerome. I wanted to be at the place where things made sense. Damn. I wanted something that wasn't lonely. I wanted to make some place where people could wake up to it, whatever the hell 'it' is. Wake up Blacksmith. We are all looking for the same damned thing. I don't know what it is. You tell me." Suddenly he was striding over toward where Bobby and I sat in the hearse. "You tell me. What the hell are those two boys sitting in? Is that a gawddamned Cadillac you keep fixing up or is that the same damned kewpie doll we are all trying for? Maybe this cuts close to the bone, and maybe I am just some foolish old man, some basket case that people laugh at or avoid, but why don't you tell me what that Cadillac is doing over there. I'll tell you what it's doing. It's over there because it's the last thing Henry was working on before he left that first time. Come hell or high water, every time that son of yours blows back into town from somewhere halfway around the world you make damn sure that you have taken it a little bit further, fixed it up a little bit more. What are you going to do if he doesn't want it Jerome? It's no good to you alone and we both know it. I'll tell you what you'll do. You'll look around for the highest bidder. And I am still not talking cash value. You're going to look around for someone who can drive it the furthest and the best. You're going to look around for the one who can take it to the places you don't have the gawddamned strength or the gawddamned time to get to yourself. And when you find him you'll pay him to take it if you have to."

The shop was dead silent. Mr. Barstow said nothing. I turned and looked at Bobby. He was not frightened. He was sitting bolt upright and he was as tense as I had ever seen him, but he was not frightened. Mr. Barstow's voice should have seemed loud after the silence, but it did not.

"Rod, you make as much sense as any man I have ever known. But for some reason, and it might be the best reason in the world for all I know, for some reason you are also the biggest fool I have ever come across. Listen to me now. Listen close. Maclenan might be after what you say he's after. I'll grant you that. But you better hear this too. He is also one hardedged business man who has got himself into a hole he can't scramble out of. He is carrying a load around right now, and he is looking for someone to dump it on. I think the signs are that he is going to dump it right on you. He will do it however he can. He will do it whenever he can, and he will use whatever excuse he has to use to do it. It won't do him any good, but he is going to unload on you the first chance he gets because he is hurting and he thinks he's been screwed. He thinks you are the one who screwed him. I'll tell you something else. Most of the people in this town think he has been screwed as well, and do you know what most of them are saying?"

Grandfather was shaking his head, more from intense confusion than negation.

"Most of them, Rod, are saying Hooray for Old Caldwell. They are saying that it's about time somebody clipped Maclenan. And they are the same damned people who will be saying that you deserve it when he finally unloads on you."

Grandfather was still shaking his head. "It's a lie. That is just a lie. Any man who thinks I meant to harm George

Maclenan is a fool or worse. Never in my life have I tried to cheat a man. I didn't even try to make money out of the sale of the hardware. Damn, you know I wasn't in it for the money. Who is saying these things? Gawddamn, the year before I sold it I cancelled half the debts in this county."

"That tears it." Mr. Barstow was completely shocked. "Yep. Right there. That tears it. Good Lord Rod, don't let that little fact get around. There is only one person in this town dumb enough to believe that you didn't cancel those debts just to screw Maclenan and you're looking at him. Nobody else would believe you in a thousand years. Not in a hundred thousand. And you don't even realize what you just said, do you? Jesus on a jackass. I have seen you like this before Rod. You are up to something and you are going to be tap-dancing up and down Main Street until you get it all figured out. I know you. But you are dancing on the tracks, Mister." Suddenly it was Mr. Barstow who was up and moving. He strode straight out of the shop. Bobby and I craned our necks out of the side door of the hearse to watch him. Neither of us had ever seen him move so quickly. He paced right out into the sunshine at the centre of the street and then wheeled around abruptly and headed straight back for the shop. He stopped dead in front of Grandfather, grabbed at his cowboy hat to resettle it, then took it right off and pointed it accusingly at Grandfather. "Rod, you are dancing on the highway and you are going to get knocked flatter than a highway dog."

I had never seen Mr. Barstow so upset, and judging from my grandfather's expression, neither had he. As he sat looking up at Mr. Barstow, slowly, almost imperceptibly, his look of surprise began to change into a smile. In any other circumstance I would have been sure that whoever Grandfather was smiling at had just walked into a trip-wire he had set up earlier in the conversation.

"A highway dog, Blacksmith? That is not bad at all. Flatter than a highway dog. Yep, for a blacksmith that is not bad at all. You know I figure I could use that one myself sometime."

Mr. Barstow put his hat back on his head, walked back to his chair and sat down. "Well Merchant, I don't recall any rule that states you have the monopoly on all the good lines. Sure, you go ahead and use it any time you want. The way I see it working out, you are going to need all the help you can get. With you starting to hop around Main Street like you did earlier this year with the relocation of the Municipal Office, I figure you will have the whole town out and watching you, waiting for you to fall flat on your grinning face. Just what are you smiling about anyways?"

"You figure that's how it's going to be, do you?"

"Yep. That's what I figure."

"I'd have to say that for a blacksmith you are usually fairly right about things. But I can't say that it bothers me anyways. It kind of puts me in mind of a circus my brother John took me to when I was a boy. If the heat has died down in here, I might just tell you about it."

"Sure, the fire's out. I should realize that you don't listen to sense anyways. You are going to tell me about this circus sooner or later. It might as well be now."

Mr. Barstow went over to the pop cooler, "Do you want a beer?"

Grandfather settled back in his chair and began to speak. "I must have been about the same age as these two here, maybe younger. It wasn't much. A long grass circus, up from Maine or maybe down from Montreal. We heard about it and walked over. It was my first time. They had the works, a couple of mangy lions, some trained dogs, clowns, a highwire act. Everything they could pack onto a couple of boxcars. It was as many people as I'd ever seen in one place, but I guess I was expecting more, because I think I was a bit disappointed. Every kid probably is.

"The item that really caught me was the highwire act. He kept looking like he was going to fall. It scared me. I was

44

just a boy. There were a couple of fellows behind us who kept calling the whole thing down. They told each other and anybody else who would listen that it was all fake. They said there was no risk at all. The one fellow said to his friend that he figured they waited until everyone was looking up at the highwire and then sent the clowns around to lift everyone's wallet. I guess there is somebody like that in every crowd.

"It seemed like the fellow up on the wire had finished when the ringmaster called out for everyone to be quiet. He said the fellow was going to blindfold himself. The ringmaster pulled out an accordion and started playing some old waltz. I think everyone was a little bit uneasy, even the two fellows behind John and me. Well, you guessed it, that son of a bitch whirled across that highwire like he was waltzing on a ballroom floor, twirled around three and four times and then danced back the other way just for good measure.

"It was about a four-mile walk home, and plenty of time for me to think about what I'd seen. I started asking John what would've happened if the fellow had fallen. It bothered me, and the more I thought about it, the more bothered I got. It got into my head the way things used to when I was that age. I kept asking John about every five minutes, 'What if he'd fallen?' You know I think part of me wanted to know he could have fallen, and part of me wanted just the show. My brother John could talk the bark off a tree, but he knew an important question when he heard one. He didn't say anything to me until we got down around Frenchman's Bend. We were about a mile from the house, just where you could see the water. He walked over to a rail fence by the side of the road there and sat up on it. I climbed up beside him.

"I guess it must have been moon rise. It seemed we could see clear out to the Island. We didn't say anything for a while. Then he started talking. 'Rod,' he said, 'there are some fellows, like those two behind us, who are always going to think that the only reason anyone does anything is just so he can get his hand in your pants. And there are some who are always going to watch for the fellow to fall, and maybe even want it a little bit. I guess you are not either kind. There is a third kind of fellow who is just going to say what if he falls and spend a lot of time worrying about it. Think about it, Rod. You know damn well what happens if he falls. The man is 20, maybe 25 feet in the air, and what with the lions and the poodles and the people, that field was packed down pretty hard. The man is naturally going to hurt himself. It's as simple as that.'

"Then he paused. John was better with a pause than anyone I ever heard. He looked over and said, 'Here's the real question Rod. Why the hell is he up there taking that risk in the first place? That is the poser Rod. Why the hell does he do it?'

"I guess I must have had a rare look on my face when he said that, because he threw his head back and laughed so hard he damn near fell off the fence. When he finished laughing he said, 'When you figure that one out Rod, you let me know, because I figure you will have the answer to the whole show.'

"You know I thought about that question on and off for quite a few years now. The first time I figured I had it answered I thought he went up there because that was how the man made his living. I was farming then, and I thought what the hell, it's no crazier way to make a living than some of the farmers north of here trying to make a living off that rocky ground around Skylar.

"That answer lasted until when I first came in and built the hardware, then I found another answer. The store gave me a scare or two that first year, and I thought maybe I should've never left the farm. It came to me that that fellow must've been up on that wire because that was the only thing he knew how to do and as crazy as it was at least he had the sense to hold onto it. Then, maybe five years ago, I found the third answer. The man goes up there because it's what he does best. Maybe he has tried a few other things, but he always ends up coming back to what he does best.

"They're all good reasons, but if you put them all together they still don't come close to the one I finally came up with. When you get old you get lonely. You get smart or you get religion. Once in a while you get an answer." He paused and leaned forward. "He goes up night after gawddamned night because of what I saw happen to that crowd when he danced across that wire. Every man, woman and child in that tent sucked their breath in at the same time. Damn. It's a wonder the canvas on that tent didn't pull in ten feet. They were all looking at the same thing. For a minute, maybe two or three—it doesn't matter how long—they were all looking in the same damned direction at the same damned thing. You tell me, Blacksmith. How often does it happen? In church? Not too damned often, maybe a birth, maybe a funeral. Big things like that, but that's about it. Birth, death and some damned fool risking his neck. But for just that moment we were all together. And everyone of us was right there. If you know anything bigger Blacksmith, you tell me about it. Every man, woman and child, stranger or friend, it didn't matter. Gawddamn, it's a wonder that tent wasn't blown off its poles when we let that breath out. Do you hear what I am saying Blacksmith? Do you?"

Grandfather was leaning forward and staring straight at Mr. Barstow. Mr. Barstow looked out toward the street and then back at Grandfather. "I hear you Rod. You're telling me that if they want to laugh, they can laugh. If they want to grab onto their wallets, they can do that too. But one way or another you are going to get them all looking in the same direction. I guess I've been hearing you. Maybe I even agree. But I've got one more question. Maybe that brother of yours would ask it if he were here. What do you do with all those eyes once you have got hold of them?"

Grandfather looked out at the street. "I don't know Jerome. Let me catch them first. Maybe if they can get together in one way, they'll see it's possible in others. What the hell, I never said there wasn't a certain amount of uncertainty involved."

Mr. Barstow resettled his hat. He started to smile. He shook his head and then he started to laugh. "The Daring Young Man on the Flying Trapeze. Who'd believe it? You pull it off Rod and my hat will be off to you. Let's get down to it. Just what particular high wire are you planning to string out over this town?"

That day Grandfather outlined his plan for a Sand Processing Plant to Mr. Barstow, and in the following days he began to outline it for the citizens of Union. As impossible as the mixture of Mr. Barstow's metaphors was, it was accurate: Grandfather began to tap-dance up and down Main Street like the Daring Young Man on the Flying Trapeze. He accosted people on street corners and harangued them about the Sand Processing Plant. Like a one-man Salvation Army Band, he performed for the regulars in front of the hotel. He called to people from the verandah as they walked down the street, inviting them to sit down and chat; having snared them, he delivered his monologue. On the pretext of small shopping errands he visited the merchants one by one, and leaning earnestly over their counters, he described the bright future he saw for Union and the Sand Processing Plant.

He developed slogans: the sands of time have run out on apathy in Union; concrete can be the foundation of economic stability for Sortie County; we laid the foundation in the first 50 years, now let's build the building; we must cement the economic prosperity of Union; think of five uses for concrete and you have five good reasons for the Sand Processing Plant. My personal favourite was: Nature manufactured it, all Union has to do is deliver.

For the first few days it worked, or at least it seemed to work. The townspeople were amused; old Rod Caldwell was on again. Each morning he continued his mysterious labours in the dining-room, making note after note in the three ledgers he kept in a drawer of the sideboard. If the door was slightly open, the picture he made sitting there was impressive. To arrive upstairs in the morning and see him there, peering into a dictionary, a cup of coffee beside him and his ledgers spread ponderously about, was to see an advertisement for dedication. If he were a great historical moment it would have been called Burning the Midnight Oil or Courting the Muse. Although I harboured a suspicion that the whole performance was just another of his guerilla tactics, even I would be taken in by the vision. Jennifer and Bobby were completely convinced, and if he was still *in camera* when they arrived in the morning, they would be all tiptoes and whispered conversation.

After a while, however, the people of Union began to tire of his performance. The replies he received on the street became more and more non-committal. By then, I had already grown tired of the whole thing. Being his companions on many of his journeys, Bobby and I heard the same lines repeated over and over again. At first I was interested because I could detect the way in which he polished and refined his material. If a particular line of argument, or even a particular line, had success with one person, he would immediately refine it and try it out on the next person he encountered. However, after half a dozen changes, even the variations began to bore me.

Just about the time my interest began to flag, I noticed something else. He did not seem to want to do anything about his Sand Processing Plant except talk about it. One or two people, Mr. Barstow, Mr. Coffey the printer, a few others, were actually interested enough to ask him for particulars about how he was going to proceed. When faced with such inquiries, instead of becoming more particular, he became, if anything, more general. Pressed, he would say, "Don't worry, I sit in that dining-room every morning taking care of precisely that kind of detail. Washing and drying the sand (or whatever the question had been) is the least of our worries at this point. Right now I am concerned

49

with staffing. I have to get the whole thing cleaned up and typed down. Rome wasn't built in a day, you know. Damn, even Union took a few years." But no-one, not me or my grandmother or Bobby or Jennifer-Rose, was granted even a glimpse of what was written in the three green cloth-bound ledgers in the sideboard. Grandmother said they contained records of the farm and the hardware and whatever else he had deemed worthy of keeping over the years, and if he ever wanted anyone to see them, he would let us know. She made it clear to me that until that time, if it ever came about, their contents were none of my concern. It was not until near the end of the whole affair, on the Saturday of the On-Site Examination, that I began to understand what was really taking place.

I am not sure what I expected from a First-Hand Assessment or an On-Site Examination, but after he had talked about it for two days, what took place was not what I expected. Grandmother packed us a lunch, and Grandfather, Bobby and I drove out to the Sand Hills. We parked in front of a farmhouse that had been owned, Grandfather told us, by a man named Kreuger Henson. It was a small two-room house that had been perfectly stripped of absolutely all of its paint by the wind and the sand. The house was on what turned out to be a small promontory, and while we sat in the car in front of it, Grandfather's rhetoric still sustained the outing. The house was, he said, a perfect example of what happened when the power of Mother Nature was disregarded. What we were going to do, he said, was co-operate with the Old Girl, and by doing so avoid the abandonment and desolation of Mr. Henson's house. "He denied the fact that he had parked himself by the edge of the sea, boys. The man was born on the coast of Maine, travelled 3000 miles and all he wanted was to get away from the ocean. He figured he was finally on solid land and when that ocean of sand dunes and blow-outs rolled up to his back door it scared him so bad he just packed up and left."

50

We walked around to the back of the house and it was like standing on the edge of an ocean. Stretching out before us, appearing to approach us as we watched, was wave after wave of earth. On the top of each wave tufts of brown grass and a few stunted evergreens, bent by years of wind, took the place of white caps. The troughs of each wave, the blow-outs, were filled with faintly golden sand. The lip of each outcrop was black soil for a few inches, which changed into grey clay and then into the sand. There were no birds. There were no animals of any sort. A light wind was blowing in our faces, but there were no trees for it to blow through; it was silent. There was nothing but wave after wave of earth. There was no horizon. The sky was a whitish blue overhead, but in front of us, to the north, it grew grey and merged with the sand hills in the distance. The desolation was unbounded.

The only appropriate response to the Sand Hills was silence. Grandfather made a few remarks in a subdued tone of voice, and then he stopped speaking altogether. We stood there for a few minutes longer in uncomfortable and uncomprehending silence. Then, without saying anything, all three of us arrived at the same decision. We turned and walked around to the other side of the house. Grandfather got out the lunch that Grandmother had packed, and although it was too early to eat, it seemed like the only thing we could do. We sat on the front porch of the abandoned house and ate in silence. Once or twice Grandfather made desultory remarks about the weather and Kreuger Henson, but he did not mention the Sand Processing Plant at all. His rhetoric, slogans and one-liners would have been completely meaningless, and he knew it.

After lunch we furtively shovelled a few boxes full of sand from where it had banked up on the windward side of the house. Feeling like trespassers, we did not even bother to go down into the first blow-out to get our sample. Then, mumbling something about surveying local opinion,

Grandfather led us back to the car. We drove in silence, and it was not until we had gone two or three miles that he began to recover his voice. He started talking about the necessity of Assessing Local Opinion, and having found one serviceable phrase, he began to search out others. "Always take into account what the local folks have to say, gentlemen. They're the ones who live with the situation day by day, and they are the ones who can give you the valuable information. Sure, you take your samples and you have them analysed, but analysis will only take you so far. That's when you listen to some fellow who has been dealing with the situation on a daily basis for half of his life."

What followed that afternoon was a repetition of our first day on Main Street, only instead of walking down Main Street we drove down road after road and stopped at farmhouse after farmhouse. At each farm we were invited in, coffee was poured, cake or pie or bread and butter was placed before us, and Grandfather would launch into all of his old lines with the new audience. Indeed, occasionally he reverted back to his earlier identity as a benign grandfather and talked about showing us the sights and educating us. The day became a long succession of farm dogs, some growling, some barking, some fawning. It became a series of bright-checked oil-cloths on kitchen tables, farm wives smiling at unexpected company, and farmers, their baseball caps hung on the backs of the kitchen chairs, their faces slightly puzzled at the one-man travelling show that had erupted in their kitchens. The Sand Hills, glimpsed every now and then as we drove around their perimeter, provided a sombre and inexplicable backdrop for it all. Before we finished, Bobby and I gave up following him, and instead we sat on the fender of the car while he talked his way into a kitchen, exchanged news and gossip, assessed local opinion, made on-site examinations, put forward his sand processing project and rolled out phrase after phrase after phrase until I finally remembered where I had heard it all before.

He was playing a pretend game, and the voice I remembered was Wayne's as he exhorted us to collect every last beetle. It was a voice that I had heard before on playgrounds or from clubhouses that had just been completed. It was not a strident voice, but it was filled with exhortation. It was not a voice that demanded agreement: simple response was enough, even argument was acceptable. Above all, it was a voice that asked for recognition.

It was sundown by the time we started driving back toward Union. There was no talk in the car except for the occasional outburst from Grandfather. Bobby was in the front seat, and I think he was asleep. I was in the back seat. I cannot say that I was disappointed in my discovery that the Sand Processing Plant was in reality a pretend game that my grandfather was playing. The realization did, however, make me tired and a little confused. It was one thing to stand back from a recently completed clubhouse or a day of beetle-collecting and see it for what it was, but it was disconcerting to find the same phenomena occurring in the adult world.

Like everyone else, I should have let my grandfather's talk of the Sand Processing Plant simply dissipate, but as we passed by the Sand Hills that evening, I decided differently. In the fading light, they were softened and took on a regular, almost hypnotic quality. Grandfather ignored them completely as we drove by, but I looked out the side window at them, and then turned around and stared at them through the back window until they were no more than an indistinct horizon. I felt their attraction. After all the busy kitchens, there was an uncluttered simplicity about them that tugged at me. When I turned back around in the car and sat waiting for the first glimpse of the lights of Union, I knew what I was going to do. At the very first opportunity, I would enter the dining-room, take out my grandfather's ledgers and read what he had been writing there every morning.

When we arrived back at the house, the Feldons from

next door were sitting on the verandah with my grand-mother and Jennifer. As soon as Grandmother had been assured that Bobby and I were not starving to death, and as soon as Grandfather had accepted his scolding for keeping us out through supper, he once more slipped into his Sand Engineer mode and began regaling his audience with stories about the On-Site Examination. I sat beneath the grapefruit tree for a short while with Bobby listening, and then I stood up and walked into the house. I went to the bathroom and turned on the light and the cold-water faucet, and then shutting the door from the outside, I walked down the hall toward the dining-room.

Although I knew I did not have much more than ten minutes to study the ledgers, I paused in the doorway. The dining-room was like it had always been. The light gleamed off the porcelain in the china cabinet. The silver crown of nutcrackers and picks still adorned the sideboard as did the tray of peppermints. I stood there and wondered how the room had managed to avoid change. Then I stepped in, took one of the peppermints and put it in my mouth and went to the drawer in which Grandfather kept his ledgers. They were not books, as I had supposed, nor were they three-ring binders. Instead, the papers were clamped by the edges of the spine. They were, according to their covers, Brampton's Instantaneous Binders. They were cloth-covered, and judg-ing by their weight, the green cloth covered some sort of metal. I turned on the lamp on the sideboard, and listening carefully for any sound out on the verandah, I opened up the first one. I mishandled it, and its cover banged open on the table. The sound was as loud as the opening of a long-unused secret panel or any other fictional noise I had every read about. No-one came to investigate.

The first binder had "The Farm" written on its inside cover but beyond that there seemed to be little logic in what he had saved. The papers were of different sizes and had faded to different shades of yellow and brown. I leafed through them quickly, but I still remember some of them. I saw a yellowing letter from his father. I noticed the signature first: Your loving Father, Wallace Frederick Caldwell. I looked up and read the final paragraph:

The old farm misses you. Would you come back and visit in five or six years time when you are established. Remember that each man takes his own chances and your brother John always took more than his share. It is not your fault, and you must bear your burdens like a man.

There were receipts from stock auctions and grain sales. There was a certificate indicating in beautiful scrolled handwriting that Roderick W. Caldwell had passed the Belloc Correspondence Course in Fine Penmanship. There was the old homestead grant that he had once brought out and shown to me. At the very end there were some blue-lined pages that looked as if they had been ripped from an exercise book. The writing on them was in a large hand. One page caught my attention because at first I thought it was a poem. I think it was a composition that looked like a poem because the writing was so large.

My Dog

I have a dog.
His fur is white
around his mouth.
My father says it is
because he is old.
I think he has
just drunk his milk.
His moustache is white.
His name is Blacky.

John Caldwell

I closed the first binder. For the first time I realized that what I was doing was wrong. I was looking where I should not look. I opened the second binder. On the inside cover was a picture of my grandfather and two uncles standing in front of the hardware store. It was just newly constructed. A ladder still leaned against the wall. There was an old glass bubble gasoline pump beside them. They were smiling. The second binder was a more proper ledger with page after page of my grandfather's entries. On many pages, at the tops and in the margins, were small notes and musings. I closed it quickly. I knew my time was running out. I picked up the third binder and opened it near the middle.

I suppose I must have still believed that I would find some neatly written dissertation on the Sand Processing Plant, because at first I could not believe that the fragments and snippets that referred to it were all that could be found. I leafed through the back half twice in disbelief. It was not just the paucity of reference that surprised me, it was also its chaotic nature. In many ways it seemed like a child's exercise book. On one page, right at the top, was written "Tools for Life by Rod Caldwell." The rest of the page was empty. On the next page he had tried again: "Tools for Living by R.W. Caldwell." On the third page over was "Life's Toolbox by Roderick Caldwell." Occasionally there were two or three pages written on consecutively. One of these sections had been titled Manpower Requirements for the Sortie County Sand Processing Plant. It started out with what seemed a reasonable breakdown of how many people the Plant would employ, but halfway down the page veered into a short treatise on the proper relationship between the working man and management and the importance of a clean cafeteria, coffee breaks and conversation. Some pages were not even that coherent. I remember one section titled Questions and Answers. It seemed to be a list of possible questions that people might ask him and the kinds of replies he would make. "Question: Is the sand too pure and uniform for cement? Answer: If it is too pure, neighbour, it would be the first thing in this world that is."

Often, in the middle of a page or in a margin there would be the word Saying, underlined in red with a small homily following it. I still remember some of them. Indeed, I later heard him use one or two of them.

Saying: People might help you to get where you want to go, but you are the person who will have to live there.

Saying: The things a man carries in his pockets will tell you what he carries in his heart.

Saying: The goods a man assembles around him are either coffins or boats.

Saying: When a fellow is worried about money, the world is as faded as a dollar bill. (This was crossed out and below it was another.) When a man is worried about money, the world is as flat as his wallet and as faded as a used dollar bill.

Sometimes his sentences tailed off into brief notations and sometimes they became complex and detailed diagrams. One sentence would be crossed out three or four times, and then as if he had used up all his energy making that one sentence correct, he would stop in the middle of a thought. I looked at page after wandering page, and by the time I was through, I was embarrassed. I think I was embarrassed for both of us. And I was saddened.

Now I think I can see something of myself in those scrawled, crossed out, half-formed sentences clamped between the covers of the Brampton's Instantaneous Binders. Each morning, when he rose at 4.30, he was trying to do so many things. He was trying to make sense. He was trying to leave a legacy. He was trying to create his future. He was trying to understand his past. He was trying to hold on to his present. Early each morning, before the sun came up and whether he knew it or not, he was trying to write a story.

He was failing.

A History of Foxglove

My grandfather's story may have been floundering from day to day, but Bobby and I no longer had to flounder with it. We were learning to tell our own story, and my grandfather's adventures intruded into the Western Kingdom only as spent rumours that could be dismissed by Wolfsbane contemptuously. Indeed, Wolfsbane began to develop a great deal of contempt. I became quite carried away with this quality in his character. It was a device that I could employ at any point in the narrative when I needed to catch my breath or gather my thoughts. It worked beautifully. A dozen poison-tipped arrows could be flashing in flight toward him; he could be completely surrounded by dull-witted but determined villagers; he could be hip-deep in the fast water above the waterfall; but no matter how desperate his situation was, I could always pause and describe his contempt for the imminent peril.

He never sneered. He did not even make weak but courageous jokes about the hopelessness of his situation. Instead his normally calm expression would become even calmer, so that unlikely as it seemed, it appeared that he was simply listening for something. If the villagers were part of the problem, or even just looking on, his serenity would throw them into leaping frenzies of rage. They could have understood a sneer; a forced, brittle witticism might have earned their respect; but the perfection of contempt evident in his total disregard of the approaching danger was hard to bear. They would begin to jeer in anticipation of his almost certain demise, and even Foxglove, ever-faithful though he was, would start to worry.

At the last possible moment Wolfsbane would act: throwing his head back, he would utter a series of piercing cries and the birds of the forest would appear, expertly catching the poisoned arrows in mid-flight and carrying them back to drop on the villagers; or looking around at the tightening circle of jeering villagers, he would make one swift bold leap straight upwards, and gaining the branch of a tree fifteen feet above him, he would escape through the forest; or standing in the swift, bone-chilling mountain river, he would recognize that no-one could fight the strength of the current, and like a ju-jitsu fighter using his opponent's strength, he would swim with the current so that when he reached the waterfall he shot out over it, executing a perfect swan dive to avoid the rocks at the bottom. Emerging further downstream, he would bow gracefully, even negligently, to the dumbfounded villagers on the rocks above.

On one or two occasions, when I needed time to figure out the details of the remainder of an episode, I would actually have Wolfsbane pause and explain to Foxglove the proper way to deal with emergencies. "Be not afraid," he would say calmly to Foxglove. "Great the danger may seem, but the means of safety lie all about us. Listen, Foxglove," he would admonish, "listen. The creatures of the forest, even the trees and mountains, will provide a solution." I liked to have him speak in inverted word order during moments of great excitement. I felt that it allowed him to express emotion while retaining a characteristic solemnity. Besides being a narrative crutch, Wolfsbane's contempt also served as a balance for his great compassion, which by that point in the summer was starting to seem too good to be true.

Unfortunately his contempt also highlighted a basic problem that I had been ignoring ever since the extent of his powers had become apparent. Given the ease with which he escaped inescapable situations, it became increasingly difficult to rationalize why he always failed to track the Lonely Elk to the Far and Distant Valley. I was quite happy to ignore the whole problem. It was Bobby who finally brought it up.

We were sitting under the grapefruit tree. The town was just beginning to come out of the day's somnolence, screen doors were opening and closing, voices were calling out. I had just begun in the usual way. "One evening, after the sun had gone down but before it was dark—just like it is now, only the sky is always a deeper blue in the Western Kingdom—the Lonely Elk came down to drink at the rushing mountain river."

"Jonathan, I have a question."

"What is it?"

"It's not just because he always has to save the villagers that Wolfsbane can't track the Lonely Elk, is it?"

Once he had spoken it, the question seemed so inevitable that I wondered why he had not asked it before. I did not know how to answer. I selected one of the long, untrimmed blades of grass at the base of the grapefruit tree, pulled it loose and put the pale, yellow-green end in my mouth. I found myself wondering why it did not taste green. Then I realized that I did not even know if green had a taste. I thought of asking Bobby. He was good at tastes, and possibly the question would have diverted him. But just then the time-honoured escape of all teachers and wise men occurred to me.

"Well, what do you think?"

"You haven't said it yet, but I think it's because he is special. He is not like the other animals or Wolfsbane could track him anytime he wanted. The Lonely Elk is..." He stopped in mid-sentence, looking for the right words. I had not looked to the Elk for an explanation, and with the beginnings of interest, I pursued it.

"How do you mean? Special how? Because he goes to the Far and Distant Valley?"

"Sure, there's that, but..." I was determined to wait for what he had to say. It was probably the first time I had been in the role of listener in regard to the Lonely Elk.

"It's not so much that he goes away to the valley. It's more because he comes back. It's like he wants two things. Mum told me once that my Dad really wanted to stay with us when I was little, but he really wanted to go away too. She said it made him really lonely, wanting to do two different things. That's what makes the Lonely Elk special, isn't it? That's why he's called the Lonely Elk. Because when he goes away he wants to come back, and when he comes back he wants to go away. He is more like a person than an elk, and that's why he's special and Wolfsbane can't track him."

I leaned back against the grapefruit tree with the same surprise I always felt when Bobby stepped away and beyond me. I took the stalk of grass from my mouth, and from long habit looked upwards for the first star. I saw the silhouette of the tree branches against the sky, but in the twilight they seemed like the dark jumbled outline of a mountain range. I felt a faint, chill brush of loneliness. My grandmother would have called it a shadow on my grave. It was as if I had forgotten that the Lonely Elk could be lonely, and in remembering it, it seemed I realized it for the first time.

I looked over at Bobby. "That is just exactly what happens, Bobby. He goes into the mountains and then he wants to come out again. You're not so dumb Bobby. I don't care what anyone says. You are not so dumb by a long shot."

"Thank you Jonathan." It was almost dark under the tree, but I knew he had begun bobbing slightly and smiling his unprotected smile. I also knew that he did not really believe he had said anything that was noteworthy.

"I mean it."

"Aw, it just makes sense, that's all."

There was no use in arguing with him, and just then I wanted to be out of the shadows of the tree anyways. "C'mon. Let's go up to the roof of the Lux and look for the first star. We can do the story later."

Whether Bobby recognized it or not, he was changing. Just as the Brotherhood of the Lonely Elk had revealed a secret geography in Union, it had also unearthed another part of Bobby. He was willing to contribute more to our conversations, and there was a subtle difference in the way he moved. More often than not, he held his head up, and he had given up the habit of looking up and out from the corners of his eyes to see if he was doing the right thing. I think the same kinds of changes were happening in me. It was not that we imagined we had literally become Wolfsbane and Foxglove; it was more that their adventures lent a grace and glamour to ours.

We did have our own adventures. We planned them with a care that would have made Wolfsbane proud, and we executed them flawlessly. We savoured them. One afternoon we borrowed a page from my life in the city and taking the threadbare tennis ball we had found on the roof of the Lux, we rang the metal sign above the door to the Hotel bar. It was not a Coca-Cola sign, but it reverberated in an equally satisfactory fashion. We watched happily as Mr. Houghton and six of his daytime regulars stumbled out, dazed, into the afternoon sunlight.

I rewrote the lyrics to the theme song of the Walt Disney epic *Davy Crockett,* and one morning Bobby and I sang them at the Café, much to the delight of the other patrons and the rare embarrassment of my grandfather.

> Born on a countertop in Joe's Café
> Dirtiest place in the USA
> Raised on the food that is cooked on the grill,
> After every meal, you start to feel ill.
> Greasy, greasy griddle
> Down at Joe's Café.

Although Grandfather disapproved publicly, he made us sing it for my grandmother and Jennifer. Jennifer laughed, and my grandmother remarked that at least we had served the cause of truth.

We discovered that speaking into the roof drain at the Lux had the effect of throwing our voices down to street

level, and we developed an elaborate plan to drive Emmet
Timson slowly insane by speaking to him out of thin air
every day as he passed, on his way to the post office. We
decided that the most effective messages would be threaten-
ing remarks about his stamp collection, but we abandoned
the plan because of our first test of the system. We tried it
out one evening when a number of people were lining up to
view a Doris Day movie. I had told Bobby to say anything
he wished as long as it was strange enough to sound out of
place. Blithely borrowing from a conversation we had
overheard that day at Mr. Barstow's, he had said, "Doris
Day is no virgin." The ventriloquist effect worked perfectly,
but Helen Stadler, thinking one of the men in the queue
made the remark, made such a fuss that we decided any
other reports of strange remarks coming out of nowhere
might lead to discovery.

We even made a foray against Wayne and his cohorts. We
watched them enter the curling-rink and waited until we
were sure they would be sitting in their accustomed places.
We carefully crept up and taped a message to the small
access panel they used as an entrance and exit. We had
debated about what to write and had finally decided upon
"Beware. The Brotherhood of the Lonely Elk is watching
you." We cut the words out of newspapers and magazines
except for the word Elk, which we were obliged to pencil in
because it is, apparently, a little-used word. Then we crept
down the side of the building until we were just on the other
side of the wall from them and hammered on the metal with
bricks so furiously that even outside the noise was thunder-
ous. Then we retreated to the roof of the Lux and idly
watched them buzzing around town on their bicycles searching for us.

It seemed like the streets of Union were dropping into our
hands like ripe fruit. One night, looking down from the
Lux, we saw what at first looked like a pure white bird glide
across the backyard behind the Union Chronicle print shop.

As we watched, it happened twice more. We climbed down, crossed the street and carefully climbed up on the garbage cans to peer into the yard.

Sitting on the back step in the moonlight was Mr. Coffey, the publisher, editor, reporter and printer of the Union Chronicle. He was not wearing his white lab coat or his green visor. Instead he sat there in shirt sleeves with a neatly folded paper hat on his head. On one side of him was a bottle and on the other side was a pile of Union Chronicles. In between drinks he precisely folded paper airplane after paper airplane and sent them floating out into the moonlight to land gracefully on the untrimmed weeds and rest there like exotic white flowers. We watched until the yard had turned to white. Then, with the same care he had taken in making them, he fastidiously plucked each white bloom, and crumpling it into a tight ball, he dropped it into a paper bag.

Or, on any afternoon, at least a quarter of the town must have seen Stanley Briski, a retired farmer who lived in town with his daughter, walk slowly out to the east road and stare at the fields beyond. But what Bobby and I saw, tracking him from bush to bush and ditch to ditch, was far different from what everyone else saw. He had some breathing problem, and every twenty yards or so we would watch as he stopped and stared at the ground with rapt concentration. Convinced by his intensity, we would stare too. Then he would look up into the sky, and we would follow his gaze. Twenty yards by twenty yards, he moved toward his destination, until by the time he reached the far side of the east road, we understood that something of great importance lay beyond. We would look with him, impressed and unsettled by the mystery of the horizon.

Or any weekday afternoon at 5.30 we could silently and invisibly track Mr. Brot, a teller at the bank, on his way home from the bank. And every afternoon, after he had purchased his quart of milk at Elliot's, he would walk through the hotel parking-lot. By the caragana hedge, protected from everyone's gaze but ours, he would tuck his quart of milk under one arm, and put his change in his wallet. Then, undoubtedly from years of habit and practice, he would lift all the bills from his wallet with his thumb and forefinger, snap them out in a fan, snap them back in line and tuck them back into his wallet so that for a moment he was some sort of fictional riverboat gambler. Placing his wallet back in his suit jacket, he would once again become responsible, respectable and dignified. Stepping out from behind the hedge, he would continue on his way home.

The bravado of four-year-olds brandishing themselves against town cats, each other and imaginary enemies was mysterious. Jimmy Simpson's habit of crouching down and making four frog-like leaps whenever he passed in front of the Feldon's house was mysterious. Mrs. Roget, raising up her skirt and scampering across the railroad trestle like a girl every time she returned to her home in the River Hills was, for Bobby and me, intimates of Wolfsbane and Foxglove, a thing of mystery.

We came to know the town's collections. Helen Stadler's husband kept a bottle in the wheel-well of his car beneath the spare tire. George Maclenan had a whole back shed filled with empty beer bottles. Mrs. Rose, the woman who lived across the street from my grandparents, had a small animal graveyard underneath two low-growing pines in her back-yard complete with small wooden crosses on which had been scratched the names of dead pets. Mr. Macphail, her next door neighbour, usually only seen swinging languorously in his hammock in the afternoons, came out every night to the darkness of his back porch where he would sit waiting, pel-let gun in hand, carefully notching his bannister with a bowie knife after every high-leaping, cat-spitting score.

Not all of the world co-operated. While George Maclenan no longer frightened me as he had on the first day, he still confused me, and I could not understand his relationship to my grandfather. There was a force in him, anger, perhaps desperation, which still made me feel very young. Helen Stadler remained as smooth and blank as a wall. Nevertheless, she recognized Bobby and I were changing. One day, instead of ignoring us as she usually did, she stopped us outside the Café and spoke to us. We had left Grandfather at Mr. Barstow's, and that was the first thing she noticed. "Well, are you out today without your chaperone?"

"Yes ma'm." As far as I can remember, I never said "Yes ma'm" to anyone. With Mrs. Stadler it came to me naturally.

"Now Jonathan, are you letting on you really know what a chaperone is?"

"It's a person who makes sure you don't do anything wrong."

"Yes it is. Good for you. If you are smart enough to know what a chaperone is, then you can be the young Scott boy's chaperone for today." She was not talking to us. In a curious way, she sounded a bit like my grandfather. She was trying out a new line on us to see how it sounded. She did not care if we were there or not. She was not even really looking at us as she spoke. "Given your grandfather's rather flamboyant obsession with the Sand Hills, perhaps a twelve-year-old is better suited as a chaperone anyways."

"Bobby doesn't need a chaperone. Neither do I. We just came down for a milkshake."

She almost seemed surprised to find us standing in front of her. "I hardly think, Jonathan, that you are a good judge of who needs direction and who does not. Now you go inside and have your soda and see that neither of you get into mischief."

No sooner had we watched her move off and turned to go into the Café than we met Wayne Maclenan and Patrick Stadler coming out. Wayne stood directly in front of us. "So, how is the Brotherhood of the Lonely Jerks?"

He had taken to calling us the Brotherhood of the Lonely Jerks after we had left the message at the curling-rink. It was a rather nice turn of phrase, and I felt at a loss for a good reply. I hit upon the one thing that was probably annoying him more than anything else.

"You can call it what you want, Wayne, but you don't even know what it is."

"So who wants to know. Just keep out of our way."

I stepped by him. "Come on Bobby, let's go inside."

He let me by, but stepped back in front of Bobby. "Well, if it isn't our old friend Wormy. Watch out Wormy or you'll trip." Bobby tripped over Wayne's outstretched foot. "Gee I'm sorry Rubber Boy, I didn't see you."

Bobby stood up beside me. He said nothing, but he was not wavering apologetically for tripping. He was not even looking at the ground. Wayne noticed it as clearly as I did.

"Jeez Rubber Boy, I said I was sorry. Aren't you gonna forgive me?" Bobby said nothing. Wayne's face darkened. I had read about peoples' faces darkening with anger, but I had never seen it before. He grabbed Bobby by the shoulder of his shirt. "Think about this, Wormy. When Jon-athan here is gone back to the city, the Brotherhood of the Lonely Jerks is gonna be even lonelier." He and Patrick laughed and walked off.

Inside we sipped our milkshakes in silence, and for the first time I realized how fragile the Western Kingdom really was. I suspect that Bobby was thinking many of the same thoughts. That afternoon I decided that I would delve into the history of Foxglove.

The History of Foxglove was notable in the annals of the Western Kingdom for a number of reasons. Not only did I prepare for it more thoroughly, but it was not just the result of robbing the appropriate parts of other stories that I had read. The reality that Bobby and I faced in Union had started to dictate how the story would grow. And yet, at the same time, it was the only episode that included any suggestion of the supernatural. Foxglove's history came to me with great ease. I had it roughly plotted out in my head when I began it, but I had assumed I would take two or three episodes before it ripened fully. Instead, detail after detail seemed to drop into place of its own accord. That evening it almost seemed like I was listening to my own story.

Foxglove's history was very straightforward. He had been born and raised in the very village that bordered the forest of the Western Kingdom. He was an orphan. Both his father and mother had disappeared shortly after his birth. No-one knew for sure where they had gone, but there had been rumours that they had discovered the secret pass to the Far and Distant Valley. For unknown reasons, they had decided to leave the infant Foxglove behind. Such circumstances would have put him in an unfavourable position with the narrow-minded villagers right from the start, but it would not have resulted in him becoming the outcast he eventually became.

His real problem was that the villagers had a deep mistrust of anything that was out of the ordinary, and right from the moment of his birth Foxglove had shown signs of a special power. Even in his cradle he had, on occasion, shimmered slightly, as if not really sure of the physical form he had taken. The superstitious villagers had immediately set him apart.

What Foxglove and the villagers did not know was that he had it within his power to change his shape at will. Nevertheless, to survive in the midst of the hostile village, Foxglove unwittingly honed his shape-changing ability as he grew up. He never literally changed shape in front of anybody; his power was far more subtle than such abracadabra, I explained, and he could not have done so even if he had wanted to. Instead he concentrated on modifying his appearance by means of his mannerisms and postures. It was almost as if he could don a disguise at will, and it meant that he could be whatever any particular villager wanted him to be at any particular moment, thus assuring that he could continue to live in the village. In effect, he was a master at blending in with his surroundings. At times it almost seemed like he was invisible.

This adequate but unsatisfactory arrangement continued for many years until one day Wolfsbane arrived upon the scene. Anyone who knew of Wolfsbane's great compassion would assume that he would rescue Foxglove and take him to live in the freedom of the forest. The reality of the situation, however, was much different. In fact, at the beginning of their partnership, it was Foxglove who rescued Wolfsbane, rather than the other way around.

The Master of Tongues had one great flaw. His weakness stemmed from the very same source as his power: his command of languages. In the forest this ability to understand all of the creatures around him was very useful, but in the village dogs barked, cats meowed, doors slammed, people shouted and laughed and cried and sang and made every other conceivable noise. Trying to listen and understand these many different voices at once completely incapacitated Wolfsbane. The first few times he visited the village he was fortunate because it was relatively quiet. By means of intense concentration he was able to procure the few supplies he could not find in the forest—salt, scholarly books on nature, and the like—and then quietly leave. On the third visit, however, he arrived on the night of the villagers' yearly celebration when they would light a giant bonfire in the village square and spend the entire night laughing, talking, drinking and telling outlandish lies to each other about their prowess in the fields and forest. Before Wolfsbane realized what was happening, he became completely frozen by the volume of sound. Foxglove, ever on the outside of such festivities, happened to be coming up the darkened street and noticed Wolfsbane standing almost in a trance just outside the fire's light.

Because he felt no need to change his appearance in Wolfsbane's presence, Foxglove knew immediately that he was dealing with an individual who was far from ordinary. After staring at him for a time, he approached him cautiously and asked if he could be of assistance. Wolfsbane, because of the years he had spent studying all he could find about the Far and Distant Valley instantly recognized Foxglove for what he was. He spoke to him in the ancient language of the Shape-changers in which he had taken care to become expert before venturing into the forest.

"Oh Brother of the Chameleons, lead me from this place or I shall perish in this confusion of noise."

Foxglove was puzzled, to say the least. He did not know that he was a member of the proud and ancient lineage of the Shape-changers. He did not even understand the language that Wolfsbane was speaking.

"I cannot understand the language you speak to me, stranger, but try to tell me what I can do to help, and I will do my best."

Wolfsbane began to see the nature of the problem, and he switched into everyday language. "You are different, Chameleon Brother, from the rest who live in this place. Whether you know it or not, you do not belong here. Lead me from this place, and we will return to the forest. We will follow the Lonely Elk to the Far and Distant Valley where only the best and truest live and where all wishes are granted. There you shall surely remember who you really are, a Shape-changer."

The sound of the word Shape-changer, which Wolfsbane uttered in the ancient language, acted almost like a spell upon Foxglove. Taking Wolfsbane by the hand, he led him out of the village and into the relative silence of the forest. Once there, Wolfsbane's mind cleared. "Pah," he said, "their mouths are full, but their minds are empty. How is it you came to live among them, Brother of the Chameleons?"

It was then that Foxglove told him the story of his life in the village. Wolfsbane immediately understood the whole situation. He correctly surmised that Foxglove had been left in the village by his parents simply in order to develop his shape-changing ability. "But now," said Wolfsbane, "you have learned your lessons well. It is time for you to leave the village. You must face this time of change bravely. Join me in the forest, and together we will search for the Lonely Elk. With his help, we shall surely find the way to the Far and Distant Valley."

As they spoke, they were sitting beneath the great tree that grew at the edge of the forest and marked where the true wilderness began. Foxglove looked back at the pin-point of dancing light from the village bonfire. Then he turned and looked into the peaceful darkness of the forest. He made up his mind. Forever turning his thoughts away from the village, he accepted Wolfsbane's offer. He was normally a taciturn individual, but that night he made a long speech.

"I will dwell here with you, Master of Tongues, and I will be your companion on the quest. You shall teach me all that you know of my people, the Shape-changers, and all that you have learned of the Far and Distant Valley. In return I pledge to perfect my powers and dedicate them to our goal and to the Brotherhood of the Lonely Elk."

And so that night Wolfsbane and Foxglove made the pact that was to bind them together, forever and ever. It was probably the most solemn moment in the entire history of their time in the forest.

It was also a very solemn moment back in Union beneath the grapefruit tree. By the time I was finished, the night had settled in around us. My grandfather had turned on the paper lanterns, and so on the side near the verandah the leaves of the tree were each precisely defined. The rest of the tree was massed with shadow. I did not know what Bobby was thinking, but I was realizing the risks I had just taken with the story. I had allowed the supernatural to enter the Western Kingdom, and it occurred to me that Bobby might well refuse to go along with it. At the same time I recognized I had cut dangerously close to reality, and I wondered if he might be angry, or even sad, that Foxglove's parents had left him or that the villagers had set him apart. I was not concerned that I had broken unspoken rules about the story; my only concern was whether it had worked. I did not look in Bobby's direction, because whatever the effect of the story was to be, I did not want to elicit feigned enthusiasm from him. I stayed still, waiting to hear his voice. Finally I leaned back and looked up into the grapefruit tree.

When I could bear the suspense no longer, I glanced over to where he was sitting. He was not there. We had practiced something we called "silent movement" to aid in our nightly journeys around town, but I was surprised that he could stand up and move away without my hearing him. I stood up, looked around and saw him standing out beside the picket fence. I walked over to him. When I came up to the fence I remained silent. He was holding onto two of the pickets. He was gripping them tightly and turning his hands as if there were jar lids on the pickets that he was trying to unscrew. He looked over to me when I came up beside him, then he looked back out to the street. I had nothing to say. Then, still staring out at the dark street, he spoke.

"It could be me, Jonathan. He could be me. I am just like he was. I know it's just a story, but I could be Foxglove." He continued turning his hands around the pickets. I wondered if he was going to get a splinter. "People never see me. They talk about me like I'm not there. But I am there. They ask my mother how I am, but they never ask me. I feel invisible. I don't fit here. Just like Foxglove." He turned and looked at me. "I thought you were just like the rest. Like Wayne and the others. No, I don't mean like them, but all the stories you told were about Wolfsbane and the things he did. But you're not like them. Foxglove is important, isn't he?"

I nodded.

"He even knows how to do things that Wolfsbane can't do?"

I nodded again.

"Jonathan?" I looked over at him. He was not crying, but it seemed he should be. "It's the best. It's the best story that ever was. It's better than the ones they read at school. It's about me. It's about me, and it's better than any of the others. It's the best that ever was."

I could hear the belief in his voice. That is all I could hear. I had angled for his belief, I had plotted for it, and it tasted sweet. In the quietness of his conviction, I should have been able to hear the villagers take one giant step closer to Wolfsbane and Foxglove, but I was not listening. Bobby could not hear or see anything but the new glimpse he had caught of himself. And I could not hear or see because I was submerged in a rush of power and mastery that was as deep and swift as the current of the mountain river that poured through the valley of the Western Kingdom.

Who Am I?

I move like the birds
I move like the fish
Tell stories without words
Whenever I wish
Sometimes I have one leg
Sometimes I have two
Only music is needed
To do what I do

Tessa Maclenan was the first fruit of the Western Kingdom. From the time that my grandfather introduced me to Tessa out by the old bandstand, I had been aware of her as a presence in Union, but without ever admitting it, I had avoided her. Then, as Bobby and I gained confidence, we began passing by the bandstand every afternoon on our way out to Grandfather's bench on the bluff. I did not admit to myself that I chose that route in order to see her any more than I admitted that I had tried to avoid her earlier. It was on the third or fourth time that I felt bold enough to try a riddle. As with the first time I had met her, she was practising her *demi-pliés,* appearing and disappearing behind the railing.

As always, she said hello. I think I almost continued along on the path, but then I stopped. In a rush, as if I were braving cold water and wanted to get it all over at once, I spoke. "I have a riddle if you want to hear it. You said you liked riddles and this one is easy but if you want to hear it you can try it."

For a moment she stopped her up and down cadence and paused above the railing. It was the first time I had really spoken to her since we had first met, and she probably wondered if I always spoke in such a hurry. She began her movement again, but as she did so she spoke.

"Sure."

"Right now?"

"Sure."

I spoke the riddle carefully and slowly. It fell in with the tempo of her movement.

"Sometimes I roll
Sometimes I run
I'm very small
When I am young
But then I grow
Both long and wide
Till I'm hard to see
From side to side
You may think I'm old
But take my advice
I'm always new
And never seen twice."

I half expected her to answer immediately. When you know the answer to a riddle, it always seems obvious. She said nothing. She continued to appear and disappear, counting as she did so. When she reached 50, she stopped, straddled the railing and leaning her back against the column that supported the roof, asked me to repeat the riddle. After I repeated it, she looked over our heads for a while. Then, just as I was starting to feel foolish, she spoke.

"Most things are small when they are young, aren't they? I mean when you compare them to how they are when they get older. Except pencils." Before I had time to say anything, she continued. "What do you like best about riddles?" She seemed to be talking to me.

"I guess I like getting the answer."

"What do you like best, Bobby?"

He answered immediately. "I like listening to them."

She considered both of our answers. "You know what I like best? I like the wondering. I like the answers, and I like listening to them, but I like wondering what the answers will be most of all. You guys go out and sit on the bench, don't you?"

We nodded.

"Can I come?"

"Sure."

"Then wait a second. I have to get my pants on." Bobby and I were both dumbfounded. She picked up a canvas shoulder bag and pulled out a pair of jeans. I had an awkward moment until I realized that she was going to slip them on over her leotards, but I liked her for being casual about it.

When she had her jeans on she vaulted over the railing. Walking her bicycle beside us, she went with us toward the bluff. It seemed she had already forgotten the riddle, and I was trying to think of something else that would be suitable for conversation. I noticed that she had a boy's bicycle, and I decided to ask if it was an old one of her brother's. When she answered, she sounded slightly defensive. "I asked for a boy's bike and this is what I got. You know why?"

Happily, I did. "They balance better, and the frame is stronger with the bar straight across."

She was surprised. "That's right. I guess you know more than riddles."

I was inordinately pleased, and I was trying to think of some casual way to mention that I was a world authority on bicycles when we stepped out of the poplars and onto the bluff. As always, there was a pause when we stepped out of the trees and looked up the river valley. As we stood there, she spoke again.

"I'm hard to see from side to side. A lot of things are hard to see from side to side. Is that really a fair clue? I mean it's not just hard to see from one side of a wall to another. Sometimes it's impossible."

For a moment I wanted to protest my honour as a riddle connoisseur, but I decided on a simple answer. "The riddle says hard to see, not impossible."

"Okay, you're right. Don't tell me the answer. I hate it when people tell me the answer."

Being accused of an unfair clue was one thing, but being accused of blurting out an answer was another. It was a point of pride to me that I would never offer or ask for the answer to a riddle, and it had made me unpopular on a number of occasions. Before I could say anything, however, Bobby made his first contribution to the conversation.

"Everything has sides." He was smiling and bobbing and enjoying himself thoroughly. Tessa was struck by his comment, and she stopped walking.

"You're right Bobby. Everything does have sides. People, houses, the moon has a dark side, streets, arguments. I can't think of anything that doesn't have sides." She started walking again and joined Bobby in his smiling. Although I could not see the cause for joy, I began to smile as well.

"You see? That's exactly why I like riddles." She was

excited. "That is just what I mean about not knowing the answer. It's wondering what the answer is that's the best. Have you ever been lost? Not knowing the answer to a riddle is like being lost. I've been lost. It's really great. Two years ago my whole family got lost." We reached the bench and sat down. With no hesitation at all, still talking, Tessa sat down between us. "It was really nice. It was the first time I ever saw the ocean. We were on vacation and mostly it was stupid, the vacation I mean, but the ocean made it really nice. It was the best on the second last day we were there. That's when we got lost. Mom and Dad were really upset. We were looking for some place that my mother heard about from Lillian MacPherson's mother. I can't remember what it was, some gift shop or antique store shaped like a giant salmon. Anyways, we got lost.

"We ended up on this gravel road. Mother had started in about how nice it was to end a holiday lost in the backyard of nowhere and things like that. Dad started to drive about 90 miles an hour." She leaned back on the bench between Bobby and me, put one hand on an imaginary steering-wheel and rested her other elbow out an imaginary car window. She was a natural mime. Her voice became very deep, and imitating her father, she continued the story.

"'Irene, I have been driving on gravel roads all my life. I was raised on gravel roads, Irene'—he always does this whole speech about gravel roads because he used to make them until he bought the hardware—'I was raised on gravel roads. My mother weaned me on gravel. I did not get toys for Christmas, Irene, I was given gravel. Now I may not have a perfect understanding of the road system in a place I have never been before, and I may not know precisely where some rinky-dink antique clip joint is located, and when you get right down to it, Irene'—he always says her name like that when he's mad—'when you get right down it it, I may not even know why someone in their right mind would travel over a thousand miles on a holiday and then spend time looking at dusty junk that is over 50 years old. But there is one thing, Irene'—he was really mad that day because she told him not to drive so fast—'there is one thing I do know about. I know gravel roads. The car we are driving in, the clothes we are wearing, the breakfast we ate this morning, this whole vacation, all of it was paid for by my knowledge of gravel roads.'"

She took her hand off the imaginary wheel and turned to me. "Actually, you know, he's right. He really knows how to drive on gravel roads. We were really floating along. Wayne was all excited and bouncing up and down on the back seat. He was only ten. Mom had gone all white like she does. What I did was just sway along and watch all these funny little places fly by. They were just little places, but they would be all tucked away behind these really big trees. The trees are just huge out there. I would look at each house and just catch it in a blink. People stopping whatever they were doing and turning to look at the road. Dogs coming out to bark at the car, but we were going so fast it was like they were all frozen. Some places had horses. Some had a few geese in the yard. The thing is I would look at each place and wonder if it was the place we were going to. That's what I mean about getting lost. Every place could be the place you are going to, so you look at it in a really special way and you actually see it instead of just waiting to get where you are going. It's like wondering about the answer to a riddle. Everything you think of might be the answer. Do you see?"

I did see. It had never occurred to me before, but I saw she was right. For someone who thought he was an authority on riddles, it was a revelation. In the silence, I also saw how she had caught us with her story. Bobby had lifted his feet up on the seat of the bench and wrapped his arms around his knees. He was looking out west over the valley. I thought of my grandfather's mountains, and I realized that beyond them lay Tessa's ocean. Bobby spoke.

"How long were you lost?"

"The whole day." She propped her elbow out the car window once more, grabbed the steering-wheel with her free hand and continued. "'Furthermore, Irene, I am not going too fast because a gravel road, when properly graded, will hold a car. And once you realize that fact, once you appreciate that...' WHUMP!" She bounced up off the bench and stood in front of us. "The road just disappeared. We came over a little hill and the road just disappeared and whump we were stuck up to the hubcaps in the sand of the best beach you ever saw. It was perfect." She stood in front of us, half dancing in her excitement. "My little brother fell right into the back of the front seat, but he wasn't hurt. My father started swearing and spinning the wheels until we were almost buried. Finally he shut the car off. It got real quiet. Then my mother says this really terrific thing. She says, 'Well George, you have made it perfectly clear that you are an authority on gravel roads. How are you with sand?'

"It was sort of a little inlet, and there was sand in the middle and rocks to climb on either side. There was nobody there, only later a couple of Indian kids came down because it turned out we were on an Indian reservation. We were there all day. Instead of driving around trying to see all of the civilized world in three hours, we spent the whole day on the beach. Mother went into shock when the Indian man came up and said we were on a reservation. He said he would help Dad, and they took the jack out of the trunk and a case of beer and sat down to discuss it. Me and Wayne got into our bathing-suits, and even Mom came down and rolled up her pants." She stopped, sat back down and looked at me.

"Have you ever been to the sea?"

I shook my head.

"You should go. You'd like it. It's my favourite place. Do I talk too much? Mother says I talk too much when I get going."

Both Bobby and I denied that she talked too much. It seemed to me that the afternoon had suddenly made a subtle change toward evening. It had grown quieter, or perhaps Tessa began to speak more quietly.

"In a few years when I am old enough, I am going to live by the sea. George, he was one of the Indian kids who came down to the beach—my brother was even more of a jerk then than he is now, and he couldn't believe an Indian would have the same name as my father—George said that you could live on what you get from the sea. Fish and clams and crabs and even some kinds of seaweed. Imagine, you could just go down and get your breakfast and cook it right there on the edge where the waves make it smooth. The waves are really great. They are kind of like a fire, you can just stare at them. At first they all look the same, but after a while you see that each one is different. It's like each one is new..." She stopped, looked over at me, and slowly began to smile. "It's waves, isn't it?"

"What is waves?"

"The riddle. They roll and run. They start small, or at least it looks that way. Each one is new, and you never see it again. Is it waves?"

I was just about to admit the one thing a riddle lover hates more than anything else. Waves was not the answer I had in mind, but it seemed to fit all the clues. Fortunately, before I said anything, she saved me.

"I guess you never think they're old, do you?"

"No," I was relieved but gracious. "But waves is close, I can tell you that much." I think I was trying to save her from the disappointment of a good guess turning out wrong, but to my surprise, she did not seem to care in the least. She continued talking.

"Anyways, that's what I like about waves. Each one is new and you can only see it once. Some are more green. Some are more blue. Some change colours as they go up. Some break quicker. But they all just keep rolling in. It was a terrific day, really. Even my little brother was all right and he was just ten. We stayed on the beach until the sun went down. The sun set right into the sea. It was like it just boiled into it. My father and George's father were really blood brothers by then, but I knew we wouldn't stay. I wanted a souvenir. I never wanted a souvenir before in my life, but I wanted one then. My brother always buys pennants. He has them all over his wall. My mother buys paperweights and stuff like that. She's really big on ashtrays. Once, before Dad bought the hardware, your grandfather was over at our house and he said it was the only place he had ever been where he could flick his ashes over 90% of the known world.

"Anyways, that day for the first time, I wanted a souvenir. We were all dried off and had our shoes on and everything because my mother is really death on sand in the car, which is pretty funny when you think we had been stuck in it all day. So what I did is just run back down to the beach while they were finishing packing. It was getting dark and it was better than it had been all day. If you stand right on the edge, a terrific thing happens. I wouldn't have seen it if I hadn't gone back. Just where the last part of the wave slips up on the beach, maybe just an inch of water slides up, right? Just there the light is reflected. The beach is all dark and jumbled, and out where the waves are it's so dark that all you see is a few white caps, but on that small part of the beach where the last part of the wave slips up, it's as smooth and shiny as a mirror, and it reflects the light that's still up in the sky. It's like there is this whole shining ribbon appearing and disappearing up and down the beach on either side of you. It was really beautiful.

"I could hear them calling, but it was so dark I could hardly see them. I knew if I was going to get anything for a souvenir it had to be right then. I wanted a beach stone, but I couldn't decide which one. They were all yelling at me by then, so what I did was close my eyes and step out on the smooth part and wait. I let the water go up over my shoes, and when I felt it go back down, I opened my eyes and

81

looked down. I took the first three that shined at me, put them in my pocket, and ran for the car. I didn't even look back.

"Now here is where it gets a bit weird. I didn't want to look at them. I started to take them out in the hotel that night and look at them, but then I stopped. It was too soon or something. I was afraid they wouldn't be any good. You know what I mean? I was afraid I would take them out of my pocket and they would be just normal rocks. I kept them in my pocket all the way home, and two days later when we got back to Union, I decided it was time. I got all three out and put them in front of me on the kitchen table. I thought for a second that I had made some kind of mistake and so I dumped everything out of my pockets on the table, but those three were the ones. They were really normal. I mean I wasn't going to start bawling or anything, but suddenly it was like I would never go to the sea again. Then I had an idea. No, it was more like the idea had me, because suddenly I just reached down and popped one in my mouth. I thought if they were wet that they might shine like they did on the beach. And they did, every one of them. It was really terrific. Until they dried, they looked just like they had in the sand after the wave went over. But here is the best thing. When I put them in my mouth, each one was salty, just like at the ocean."

She began rummaging in her bag. "The thing is, they still taste that way. Lillian, she's my best friend, she says that it's just because I carry them around all the time and they get sweaty, but it's not true. Do you guys want to try it? It's like hearing the sea in a seashell, only tasting it is better. When you taste it you can hear it and see it and smell it all at the same time. Hold out your hands."

She dropped a stone into each of our palms. Mine was a dull red, swirled with white. It was better than an ordinary piece of gravel because it was so smooth, but it did not seem particularly special.

"You don't have to tell me. I know they don't look like much, but when I say, we'll put them in our mouths, right? But not until I say. You have to think of waves. Are you ready?" I was starting to feel the way you often feel when someone is coming to the punchline of a joke you know is going to fail and you want to be ready to counterfeit laughter. Bobby and I nodded that we were ready.

"Okay, close your eyes."

We closed our eyes.

"Okay. Now."

I raised my hand and carefully placed the stone in my mouth. I do not know what I was expecting, but at first the only taste was smoothness. With my eyes closed, I noticed for the first time the slight breeze from the river valley blowing on my face. Then I tasted the faintest taste of salt. It came and went before I could name it. I felt the warmth of the sunlight on my face. I felt the back of the bench touching on my shoulder-blades. I heard the crumpled-tissue sound of the breeze in the grass. Then I saw them. Somewhere between deep blue and deep green, each curling white at the top, banners of seaweed rolling up their faces, wave after wave rolled toward me. Startled, I opened my eyes. Tessa was smiling. After having my eyes closed, the light seemed new. She seemed new as well.

"You saw them, didn't you? I can tell. I knew you would." I nodded. "I mean I didn't know for sure, but I thought you would. I just had a feeling. You know what I mean?"

We both looked over at Bobby. He opened his eyes and I could tell without asking that he had seen something as well.

"Now spit them in your palm and look."

I dropped the stone into my palm as if it was a peach pit or a watermelon seed. The stone shone. The sheen of saliva made it glisten with colour. It was smooth and rounded, and it was alive in my palm as it must have been alive on the beach. As I watched, it dried and faded. Tessa was speaking.

"The waves make them smooth. It takes years and years. Sometimes you can get a good skipping rock that is just as smooth down at the river."

I know that I did not stiffen or look up sharply, but she suddenly knew. She looked surprised. "The answer is river, isn't it Jonathan?"

I nodded and looked down at the stone in my palm; just then I was convinced that it had somehow provided her with the answer. I recited the riddle.

> "Sometimes I roll
> Sometimes I run
> I'm very small
> When I am young
> But then I grow
> Both long and wide
> Till I'm hard to see
> From side to side
> You may think I'm old
> But take my advice
> I'm always new
> And never seen twice"

"It's a really good riddle." We passed her stones back to her and she stood up and put them in the pocket of her jeans. For the first time that day she seemed at a loss for words. "I have to go now...I probably talked too much. My mother says I talk too much.... Anyways thanks for the riddle." She started walking away with her bicycle. Then she stopped and spoke again. "It's the first time the stones have worked out for anybody but me..." She paused again confused. "I don't mean that I try them out on just anybody or anything like that. I just thought they might work with you. That's all." She moved a bit further and then she stopped again. I had the strong feeling that I should be saying something,

84

but I could not think of anything. She spoke again. "It was a really good riddle. Maybe I'll bring one tomorrow. Okay?"

I finally gained the presence of mind to speak. "Sure. That would be great."

"Okay. Well maybe I'll see you at the bandstand at the same time tomorrow. I mean if you come I'll probably be there because that's when I practise and I'll be there. Probably for sure."

"Okay."

"I won't talk so much tomorrow." She began to ride up the rise toward the poplars, but before she disappeared into the trees she stopped again. "Say, do you guys want one?"

"One what?"

"A stone. Do you want a beach stone?"

"Sure."

She left her bike and ran back to us. "Here." She gave us each a stone. "They only work once a day. I'll see you tomorrow." She turned and ran.

Over the next few days, we continued to arrange our meetings in a carefully casual and uncommitted way, but before the week was out, we took it for granted that we would spend the afternoons together. The three of us became friends. We talked. We tried out riddles on each other; we watched birds and Tessa told us their names; I showed them bicycle-riding tricks on Tessa's bicycle; Bobby revealed a hidden talent for finding good skipping rocks and showed us how to send them bouncing across the water; we explored the bandstand and the poplar grove and the railroad trestle and the riverbank; but mostly we just talked. Anything else we did was simply a setting for the words that flowed between us. If Tessa was finishing her ballet exercises, our conversation would fall into the cadence of her movement. If we were rambling from the bandstand to the bench to the river, our conversation rambled as well. We all became expert at Tessa's free-form technique with riddles. There was

85

no headlong rush for answers; each clue became an invitation instead of a hurdle. Bobby was especially proficient at her approach. For the first time he had found a way of talking that suited his view of the world. And sometimes, with no riddle or exploration or any other activity to provide us with an excuse, we simply sat by the river and talked. The exchange of histories and present moments and futures flowed by as effortlessly as the river. Coming to, we would notice that the sounds of the river had become quieter but more distinct, and we would realize that we were all in danger of being late for supper.

It seemed that we held up every part of our world for inspection, but now I see that the current that ran through most of what we said was change. I had been aware of change since that spring, but it had been more of a scent than an idea, the smell of road tar and wet wood. That summer it became the dry, nose-pinching scent of the creosoted timbers of the railroad trestle; or the basement smell of the dew-moist earth we laid upon as we spied out at the dark streets of Union; but most of all it became the deep green, partly rank, partly clean smell of the river's edge.

For Tessa, change was more than a scent. She did not try to escape it, as I had tried. Instead, because she was more foolish, or more brave, or perhaps more deeply touched by change, time after time she tried to put words to it. I remember one afternoon more clearly than all the others. It began with her talking about a red-white-and-blue rubber ball, and before she was done she had, in her own fearless and rambling fashion, come as close as most ever do to finding the right words for it.

When we arrived at the bandstand that afternoon, Tessa was not practising her ballet. Instead, she was bouncing a small striped rubber ball of the type usually found in the hands of small children or in the mouths of dogs. She was bouncing it with the same concentration that she took to her dance exercises, and she did it with the same grace. I wondered for a moment if bouncing the ball was some new sort of dance exercise. Bobby and I were happy to watch until she noticed us. She caught the ball, and tossing it up lightly, she began talking.

"Kind of stupid, right? But I can still do them all. One Two Three A-lary, Roller Coaster, Peter Pan, Gopher Hole. You name it and I bet I can do it. Two years ago I probably could've won the ball-bouncing championship of North America."

Bobby was impressed. "Do they really have a ball bouncing championship?"

"I'm not sure, but they probably do. I would've won it if they had one. You want to see?"

"Sure." Bobby and I sat back to watch and listen.

"Okay. Each routine has a poem that goes with it. I'll do the simplest one." Standing there, framed by the columns of the bandstand and the poplars, she began to bounce the ball with one hand. Every three bounces she raised her right leg and bounced the ball underneath it. Then she began to sing. I had heard it before, and even today I could probably hear it in the local schoolyard.

"One, two, three
A-lary
Four, five, six
A-lary
Seven, eight, nine
A-lary
Ten a-lary
Catch me."

She caught the ball on "Catch me" and looked up at us. "All the routines are like that, but with Peter Pan you raise your leg and bounce the ball back under right away, and with Roller Coaster you lift each leg in turn. Roller Coaster is the most difficult." She moved to the steps and sat down. She

87

held up the ball and shaking her head as she looked at it, she said, "It's not as easy as it looks you know. Two summers ago I spent 24 hours a day just bouncing a stupid ball. Then last summer I bounced a lot, but not as much. This summer, right now is the first time. I found it under the stairs this morning when I went down to get a jar of strawberry jam for my mother."

Her voice was quiet. There was a tone to it which I could not name. Bobby spoke. "Don't worry. I'll bet it's like riding a bike. Mr. Barstow told me that you never forget how to ride a bike."

"That's not true, you know. I mean it may be true, but it's not right. Maybe you don't forget how, but you forget. Everybody forgets. Look at it." She tossed the ball out and I caught it. "Look at the cracks in it."

I did. The paint on the ball had fractured into a web of tiny lines. I thought she was concerned that it had been ruined. "It still bounces, Tessa. It doesn't matter if the paint has cracked a bit. None of it has even worn off yet."

"I know all that. I mean, I probably know everything there is to know about rubber balls. If you look at those little cracks the right way, it starts to look like a really old plate. My mother has these antique plates in the china cabinet and they have the same cracks. I must have been really young the first time I noticed it, and I thought my ball was a hundred years old. I sat down on the basement step this morning looking at this stupid ball and realized that there was a whole bunch of stuff like that I had forgotten, and if I hadn't found the ball by accident I wouldn't have remembered any of it. You don't forget how to bounce the ball, but you forget all the stuff that made it special."

She must have seen signs of confusion in our faces, or felt it in herself. She began shaking her head again. "I know. It sounds stupid, but there was a whole lot of stuff I remembered this morning about bouncing a ball. If you do a whole lot of bouncing, the ball lasts about a year. So I would be

88

bouncing a new one in the spring and not even thinking about the old one, and some next-door-dog would go by with the old one in his mouth all spitty and happy. And you never knew how he got hold of it, but you knew he was having as much fun with it as you did. Or when the paint is starting to fall off, and you bounce it first in a puddle and then on the sidewalk and it leaves those round wet circles I used to call rubber-ball tracks. That kind of stuff used to make me feel so good. There was all kinds of it. Two years ago I used to bounce every day, and when it was rainy I bounced down in the basement to keep in practice. It made a whole different sound in the basement. It kind of slaps around and the sound bounces as much as the ball. The next-door-dog, the cracks in the paint, the sound in the basement, how it felt when you did a whole series straight through twice without a mistake, that's the kind of stuff you forget. So what's the use of anything? I mean that's the best stuff about balls, and that's exactly the stuff you forget."

I hoped that Bobby had something to say, but he did not. I knew she wanted to hear something from us, but I did not know what to say. I tossed the ball back to her, and decided to try my grandfather's advice.

"Sometimes, when something is bothering me, I just leave it alone for a little while. I don't mean you ignore it. You just leave it alone for a while. Sometimes I think about a thing too much. My mother calls it worrying a bone. My grandfather says you should just bury it for a while and let it soften up."

"You do that too? My mother calls it being excessive. She has said that to me ever since I can remember. Don't be excessive, Tessa. She said I was being excessive that summer with the ball. I was ten years old. You know what I said to her? She thought I was really cute and she repeated it to everyone. I said I was going to bounce a ball until I was sixty. I meant it, but the funny thing was that at the same time I said it, I knew I was going to stop. All the other girls did. Each year it was someone else. That year it was Mary Stern. I'm not talking about dolls or playing house or any of those things. I'm talking about skipping rope or kick-the-can, or bouncing balls. They're good things, and you shouldn't have to give them up just because you get older.

"Why do people forget that stuff? No matter who it was, sooner or later, she gave it up. I would be bouncing my ball on the front step and Mary Stern would come walking down the street and she would be going to the café or going down to look at clothes or thinking about something and I'd call out to her. She would look up and not even remember that just the summer before she loved bouncing a ball as much as me. But suddenly I was just some little kid bouncing a ball on the front step, and it was like she had trouble even remembering my name. It's all too stupid to even talk about." She stood up. "Let's go out to the bench." She walked by us, still tossing the ball up and down, and started out toward the bluff.

I would like to think that Bobby and I remained quiet because we were impressed with the gravity of the subject, but the truth of it was that we had come to understand Tessa's way of talking. It was as if she had to hear her thoughts spoken out loud before she could begin to make sense of certain subjects. We understood that we were necessary in the process as clearly as we understood we did not have to say a great deal. As always, stepping out of the poplar grove changed our mood. Immediate concerns disappeared into the distance before us. That day we wandered to the bench and from there to the riverbank. It was not until we had come back up to sit upon the railroad trestle that the subject of the rubber ball returned. She absently pulled it out of her bag and began tossing it up in the air once more.

"You know, I was so crazy that I even used to look at people and think I knew which ones would be good at bouncing a ball."

"That's not crazy. I used to do that with people and bikes.

I even had names for them. There were coasters and peddlers, and wing handlebars and fenderless and others like that. When I got a chance to see them on their bikes, it usually turned out that I was right."

"That's right. I was the same with ball bouncing." She looked at the two of us appraisingly. "You and Bobby would do all right. I remember thinking that your grandfather would be doing Roller Coaster inside of a week if he ever got started." I tried to think of him bouncing a ball. It seemed entirely possible.

Bobby spoke with great certainty. "Mr. Barstow could."

Tessa thought for a moment. "You're right. He would just stick to One Two Three A-lary, but he would have a lot of fun. I'll bet your mother could too, just like that."

Bobby was smiling. "Mrs. Stadler couldn't."

Tessa agreed again. "You're probably right. Neither could Mrs. Elliot or Mrs. Royal."

I thought I detected an inconsistency. "But Mrs. Stadler isn't old like those other two."

Tessa began to smile. "But she's really stiff."

Bobby stood up, giggling. He had picked up Tessa's habit of occasionally miming instead of speaking. Standing on the railroad ties and wobbling slightly, we could see him trying to bounce an imaginary ball while looking out of the corners of his eyes at it. It was a clear picture of Mrs. Stadler. "She would try to do it without looking straight at it, and she would keep missing."

We laughed. I spoke up, trying to catch some of Mrs. Stadler's diction and inflection while Bobby continued to mime her. "Well, it certainly does bounce, doesn't it? I do not think, however, that we could describe this as a useful activity." In between eruptions of laughter, Bobby and I continued to clown with the thought of Mrs. Stadler bouncing a red-white-and-blue rubber ball. By the time we subsided, Tessa had grown sombre again. We watched the river quietly for a while, and then she spoke.

"My father couldn't even bounce a beach ball right now. He could have two years ago, but he couldn't right now even if he wanted to." She spoke of her father only rarely. We never talked of the difficulty between him and Grandfather, and neither Bobby nor I had ever mentioned that we had listened to his drunken ramblings behind the hardware store on more than one occasion. Still, I was always interested when she spoke about him. "It's what I mean about forgetting. Things just go away. He started building me a room in the basement about a year ago. He said a young lady of my age should have privacy. He hasn't finished it. Not that I care about the room in the basement, but it's like he's forgot.

"Do you see that bridge?" She was pointing up river to where the new bridge crossed over it. "That was one of the last things he worked on when he was still working on the roads. He helped build that bridge. Usually he and Professor Erdner were off someplace far away and he would drive the car back and forth to the Professor, but when he worked on that bridge he used to just drive the Professor home."

"Professor Erdner?"

"That's what he called his tractor. I don't know why. He just called it Professor Erdner. That's what I mean about him not being able to bounce a ball anymore. He used to be funny. He made me laugh all the time. When he worked on that bridge, I would drive my bike down after supper to watch him. He always worked late. He was grading the road up to the bridge. I would sit on those cement things... pilings. I would sit on the pilings and watch him, and right near sundown he would stop and come over and sit down with me and drink the last coffee in his thermos. He always offered to share, but I let him have all if it because he was thirsty. We'd just sit there and watch the river get clear. He liked that a lot. He'd say, 'Tess, I have swallowed enough dust in my time to know that river is a pretty good housekeeper.' It was true. Right after he stopped grading the river

92

would be all brown and dirty and then after ten or fifteen minutes all the dust would be gone out of it. You never really noticed it, but suddenly it would be as clear as glass.

"That was the best time. I would look up and the whole valley would be out of the sun. But up on the edge you could see the grain elevators still had sun on their top halves. The river would go all flat-coloured. Dad would finish up his coffee and he would always say, 'it's sweetest near the end.' We wouldn't talk much, and right down on the river where we were it would almost be chilly even after a hot day. I liked to sit close to him. He smelled good. I told him that once and he said it was Dust and Diesel Number Five.

"Anyways, when the river cleared, he would sort of wake up and ask if I had the reflector on the back of my bicycle fixed yet. He knew I didn't but I would have to say no. Then he would say, 'Well, no daughter of mine is going to ride on this county's roads without a tail-light. I guess you better hitch a ride with me and the old Professor.' He would lift up my bike and set it just behind the blade and we would start up. That was the best part. The Professor was really loud, and Dad would always shout, 'Hear that Tess, more horsepower than if every horse in this county pulled together.' He really liked Professor Erdner. I got to stand up right beside where he drove and it was like riding on a chariot. The sound was really loud, but it was almost like it was a warm sound. When we drove it made a cool breeze and I would get goosebumps and put my hand out near the smoke stack where it was warm. Sparks flew out like fireflies, and it was really nice.

"Then halfway up the hill he would start shouting out this really crazy stuff. It was a game we had. He'd say, 'Efficient production Tess. It comes right after supply and demand. The old Professor here shovels it better in one hour than a hundred men could in a day.' Dad would really be shouting so I could hear him, and I would be laughing. I would shout back, Pyramids. And he would shout back, 'Three weeks work for the Professor.' I would shout, Great

Wall of China. And he would shout, 'Done before lunch.' I would shout, Panama Canal. He would shout, 'Done before coffee break.' And sometimes it was so silly that I would laugh so hard I couldn't think of any more. We'd drive up and around town on the east road and we would be shouting out all these really silly things and laughing and everyone in town would be sitting in their living-rooms doing stupid town stuff. But we drove around it all like we were on parade in this big yellow chariot and when it was cool you could just put out your hand and feel the heat from the engine and sometimes I wished we could just drive around and around town forever like the boys do on Saturday night.

"When we pulled into the yard behind the house and he shut off the Professor it was more quiet than anything you've ever heard. We would sit there for a minute or two longer. The engine used to tick as it cooled down, and I would ask him dumb questions just so we could stay there for a while longer." Tessa stopped talking. Her face darkened like Wayne's, only more sombrely. When she spoke again she was not shouting out over the noise of the tractor.

"Then he sold the Professor. Last winter he just sold the Professor. He said he wanted to buy your grandfather's hardware store. Home for supper every night, he said. No more dust for lunch, he said. What a joke. I don't think he's been home for supper in three months. And it's not just that he sold the Professor. He's changed. He always used to tell us stories of what your grandfather used to say down at the hardware. We used to sit around after supper and listen and laugh. Now you can't even mention Mr. Caldwell when Dad is in the house. He's changed. He's forgotten about all that good stuff just like I forgot about bouncing a ball." She was angry. "It's not just stuff you forget. I've thought about this. You forget yourself too. Do you remember the very first day of school Bobby?"

"Sort of, I guess."

"Well I do. That was the year Mrs. Stadler taught because

the other teacher went away to have a baby. She put me in the corner. Right on the first day. I didn't know you weren't supposed to talk. Nobody told me. I cried and started to leave, and she wouldn't let me. Nobody told me you couldn't go home either." She turned to me. "About halfway through the morning she started in on Bobby for fidgeting. I mean everybody in town knew he couldn't help it, but not old Frog Face. She told him to quit fidgeting, and he just smiled like he does and kept right on waving around. The more she yelled at him, the more he smiled and waved around. I really liked you for that Bobby. I thought it was just terrific. She got real mad and finally dragged him down to the principal. Old Crowther brought him right back down the hall and then told her off right by the door. We could all hear it. Do you remember that Bobby?"

"Sort of." He was smiling modestly and waving around.

"Was it like I said?"

"I guess so. I don't remember it all."

"That's exactly what I mean. I can't even remember who I was in Grade 1, not really. And if I am not the same person now as I was then—and believe me, Frog Face wouldn't get away with it today—then who am I going to be next year? Who am I right now? It's like the riddle about the river. I'm always new, and you just get comfortable someplace and then you change and have to start all over again. Then to top it all off, you can't even remember who you were before. Not really. Sometimes you can't even remember the things you did. Do you see? It's all too stupid for words." There was a clear anguish in her voice. She looked down at the ball in her hand as if it was the sole cause of her confusion. "I should just throw this dumb ball in the river."

I looked up the river to the bridge that her father had worked on. I realized that sooner or later it would be replaced as it had replaced its predecessor. And there would be another one after that. I looked down at the railroad ties of the trestle, and then through them to the trestle itself. I realized it would also be replaced. The wood came into focus, cracked and splintering and bleaching out. I looked away quickly. The trees on the riverbank were turning lightly in the breeze. My gaze sharpened, and I saw the leaves were innumerable shades of green, defying me to have words for them all. I looked away from the trees. I saw my own hand. One knuckle was scraped. The colours were discordant; white where the skin stretched over my knuckles; there was a faint red on the back, and tiny black hairs; there was the blue shadow of a vein; the skin between my thumb and forefinger was papery. I realized that it was not the hand that had been mine when I was younger. It seemed like someone else's hand. I let go of the railroad tie and turned my hand over with the same detachment I might have had for a dead bird. On the underside of my longest finger I saw the faint half-moon scar where I had placed it on a burner on the stove when I was three years old. I traced the scar with my thumb, carefully, lest I should erase it.

I risked a glance at Bobby and Tessa. He was still smiling in a puzzled way, and Tessa was still staring at the rubber ball. I was an unfathomable distance away from them. I blinked and stared down to the river. The water was slipping smoothly and silently under the trestle and neatly out of my line of vision. I felt a sudden vertigo. Both the river and the trestle were disappearing into the same line where my vision stopped. It seemed that everything, Bobby, Tessa, the trestle, the bridge, the trees, the entire summer were all tipping into that same cavity. I felt the trestle move. I held on tightly.

And then, from far, far away, I heard the sound of singing voices. The sound was pure and high and beautiful. I could not make any more sense of my hearing than I could of my sight, but I listened desperately. The voices sang again.

Jonathan and Tessa
Up in a tree

KISSING
First comes love
Then comes marriage
Then comes Tessa
With a baby carriage.

The words brought everything back into proper focus. I looked away from where the river disappeared beneath the trestle. Tessa was looking back over her shoulder and up toward the bluff. She called out. "I see you Dorothy Stillson and Debbie Waters, and if you don't take off right now, I'll tell your mothers that you were out on the bluff alone."

She turned back and looked at me. I watched a disconcerted look come into her face. "What are you smiling about Jonathan?"

I did not even know I was smiling, but I did not care. I smiled even more broadly. She blushed and began to smile in return. "You know, I used to call that out too. I think it's sort of a revenge when you see some older girl doing something you don't understand. It's kind of stupid, right? I mean, who ever kisses up in a tree?"

I found myself speaking. "Did my grandfather ever tell you about his tree?"

"Sure. I think he must have told everyone in town the same story. It's a good one." She was still puzzled at my smile, and my question had confused her further. I did not care. Just then it was important that I make very clear to her what had occurred to me.

"What I mean is that at least that story stays the same. Maybe not exactly, but mostly. You're right about things changing, but maybe that story doesn't. Every year since I can remember he's told me that story. My grandmother says he's told it for close to 25 years. And we all remember it the same way, or close to the same, anyways. That's not exactly what I mean. It's just that maybe if we all remember something the same way, then we'd never forget it. Then it

97

wouldn't change. Do you see?"

She was looking at me closely. "Okay, Jonathan. Thank you. I'll think about it." She smiled again. "It sounded like you were about to become excessive. I know just what the problem is. C'mon you guys, follow me."

She stood up, and we followed her out to the centre of the trestle. She held up the rubber ball. "Dearly beloved, we are gathered here today to say a fond farewell to one slightly used, red-white-and-blue rubber ball... Quit laughing Bobby, this is serious." He giggled even more and it started all of us. When we finished, she began again.

"Be serious, you guys. We have to do this together to make it right. Repeat after me. Ashes to ashes."

"Ashes to ashes."

"Dust to dust."

"Dust to dust."

She let go of the ball. It splashed into the river and then bobbed up to the surface.

"And BALLS to the river."

"And BALLS to the river." We shouted it out, and it echoed back to us. The rubber ball, its ancient, cracked-china surface glistening, floated under the trestle. We scrambled to the other side to watch it emerge. Tessa slipped, and I steadied her with my arm across her shoulders. Bobby came up on her other side, and she put her arm over his shoulders. We quietly watched the ball barber-pole red-white-and-blue as it sailed away down the river. It caught an eddy, hesitated for a moment, bobbing, then found the line of current once again and sailed beyond the long shadow thrown by the trestle, and beyond the even longer shadow of the three of us standing there arm in arm. When it finally sailed out of sight, Bobby spoke.

"You know what Mr. Caldwell told me once? He told me if you dropped something in just the right place in the current of a river, it could sail all the way to the sea."

The Dance Begins

While Bobby, Tessa and I were spending our days down by the riverside, Grandfather's Sand Processing Plant was ripening and going to seed. I was not surprised. Nor was I surprised that it ended in a confrontation with Helen Stadler. Indeed, I wonder if Grandfather had been looking for just such a situation so that he could end his crusade without having to admit that he was growing slightly tired of the whole thing himself. The only thing that did surprise me was the bitter tone of the ending.

It began calmly enough. We were sitting on the hotel benches opposite the hardware. Many of the townspeople had started avoiding Grandfather for fear of being lectured about the Sand Processing Plant, but there were always one or two old men sitting out in the sun after their glass of beer who were willing to serve as his audience. It was a good location for Grandfather because when he spied a new pair of ears approaching, he could speed up or slow down his narrative to insure that he was at an interesting point.

He did not see Helen Stadler go into the hardware that day because his back was to the street, but Bobby and I noticed her. It was one of the cardinal rules of the Western Kingdom that he and I should be as observant as possible, and we both practised diligently. We also saw her when she exited the hardware and crossed to the drugstore up the street. I knew that to go home or to complete whatever business she had on Main Street she would have to walk right by us. I wondered if Grandfather would finish before she appeared again. It did not seem likely. When she came out of the drugstore, Grandfather finally noticed her. For some reason he moved quickly forward to his dissertation of the role of wave and wind action in the creation of sand.

"Figure it this way, Wesley." He was talking to Wesley Stoller. "That is not just sand out there. What we have out there is the product of a hundred thousand years of careful manufacture by the forces of nature. It goes like this. There's wave action and wind action. I've studied it. Waves work like this." He began moving forwards and backwards. "Break break break the poet says, and that is just what happens. Those breakers come in and pulverize the rock. It's not fast, mind you, but it's persistent. And it's not just in and out. That wave pattern gives you a circular motion as well." He began waving his arms in large circles as he moved forwards and backwards. "Can you see it? It's kind of a carrying motion. Damn, you know what has just occurred to me Wesley?" It had actually occurred to him quite a few days earlier; I had heard the line three times before already. "It occurs to me that we don't just have the benefit of nature's manufacture out there. She has even provided transport. She has delivered it to our doorstep, Wesley. She hauled that sand up the edge of that ocean that used to be there, and now all we have to do is go down and play on the beach. Yep. If this community would come to its senses, we could have a sound economic venture as easy as playing sandcastles on the seashore."

"Well, Mr. Caldwell, I think such energy at your age is remarkable, but I wonder if..."

"Hello Helen. You startled me. But you have touched on the key word. Age. Age and wave action and wind action combine to create the phenomenon commonly known as sand."

"I have been hearing a great deal about your ambitious plan for the Sand Hills Mr. Caldwell. I confess the metaphor of sandcastles is rather an alarming one for any industry that is being seriously proposed, but I was just going to remark that Mr. Stoller here can't really hear you anyways, can he? Age has not been as kind to him as it has to you." She aligned herself toward Mr. Stoller, and raised her voice. "How are you today, Mr. Stoller?"

As if to oblige her, he replied, "What's that Helen?"

"I said it is a lovely day to be sitting in the sunshine."

"Oh, my hearing's not so good, I thought you asked me how I was."

A shadow of uncertainty crossed her face, but she turned back to my grandfather. "I was wondering, Mr. Caldwell, why you have not approached the town council with your plan. Main Street is, of course, a very democratic forum, but if your Sandcastle Project is what you say it is, you might describe it to the council. We are, after all, elected representatives, and the town's welfare is our responsibility."

I was probably the only one who noticed the slight insecurity that showed on his face. "Well Helen, I just might do that. I figure I have to get a few kinks ironed out first. No offence, but if you want something to slide by a town council, it has to be pretty slick."

"I confess I have wondered why you have not discussed your plan with the one man in this town who is qualifed in these matters."

Even I saw what was coming, but for some reason, Grandfather stepped right into it. "I don't know who you are talking about Helen, but I have studied the matter a fair bit, and I don't think there is anyone around here who knows any more about it than I do."

"Now Mr. Caldwell, I am sure that if you stop and think about it, you will realize there is one person you have not consulted. Indeed, he is probably the only person you have not consulted." She was very sure of her ground. There was almost a smile on her face. "Mr. Maclenan has pointed out that in all of the particulars, your plan, at least what we on the council have heard of it, is very sound." I noticed Mr. Elliott and Mrs. Royal walking across the street toward the hotel. Then I noticed that Mr. Swartz, senior, was making his way toward the coffee shop for his usual early afternoon cup of coffee. I did not know then that a crowd always manages to gather at such times.

Grandfather had started to realize what he had been set up

for. "So he thinks my particulars are pretty sound, does he?"

"Yes he does, and he is the one man in this area who has spent his life working with road construction and foundation building and other related activities. I believe his approval would go a long way toward swaying the council." She paused, and we all waited. "But for one thing, Mr. Caldwell." She paused again, completely confident that he had to ask what that one thing was. She was sadly mistaken.

"Let me get this straight, Helen. The town council has been talking about the whole project without the benefit of what I might have to say about it, and you have come up with a 'but.' Somehow that doesn't surprise me. Somehow I kind of figured that might be the case. The fact of the matter is that around here the one essential thing you have to have to sit on the town council is a 'but.'"

She tried to get her ground back. "That 'but,' as you call it, Mr. Caldwell, is in fact..."

"Yep," he turned to the slowly assembling audience. "You get one or two town councillors with those big buts sitting in judgment and..."

"BUT, Mr. Caldwell, George Maclenan has pointed out that a market survey is the one thing every amateur always forgets, and he says, Mr. Caldwell, that you do not have a market. The nearest city is much too far away to be of any use, and they have supplies of sand much closer and..."

"And one big but meets another big but and you get those big buts together and pretty soon, by gawd, they will squash anything in God's creation flatter than stale beer."

Wheezing and rattling, Wesley Stoller began to laugh. "I haven't heard a better one in two years Rod."

Helen Stadler was angry. She was very angry. "You may make silly jokes Mr. Caldwell, even off-colour jokes, but..."

"BUT, Mrs. Stadler, at least I do not discuss a man's plans without giving him the benefit of a hearing."

"Oh, we have heard. Believe me, we have all heard. That is the one thing you can count on. You spend your days making a spectacle of yourself on Main Street and wasting anyone's time who comes within earshot and in the meantime your grandson and the Scott boy, who you said you would chaperone, are sneaking around back alleys and God knows where else and all that you do is loaf around like a vagrant and talk about sandcastles and make jokes. We would be very interested, Mr. Caldwell. Yes, we would be extremely interested to give your Sandcastle Project precisely the attention it deserves. Until that time Mr. Caldwell, all I have to say is good day."

The anger left my grandfather as he watched her walk away. He put his hand up in a curiously ineffectual gesture, as if to call out to her or to brush something away. Without saying anything to us or to the others standing around, he began to walk off down the street. After a few steps, he seemed to realize where he was, and he changed direction for home. Bobby and I scrambled to catch up to him. When we came up beside him, he seemed befuddled, almost surprised that we were present. He paused and looked back at the hotel benches. I thought he was about to say something, and I waited for it confidently. I knew he would have an appropriate one-liner for the occasion.

He made the same impotent gesture with his hand, and shaking his head, he spoke. "What the hell." For the first time that summer I saw that he was very, very tired.

The day after Grandfather's Sandcastle Project was washed away, he did not accompany us downtown. Out of force of habit, Bobby and I went down without him. We stopped in at the café and then made our way back toward the house for lunch. Wayne, Patrick and Raymond rode beside us on their bicycles.

"It's Jon-athan and The Wriggler. We thought you'd be out making sandcastles with your senile grandfather."

"Or maybe mudpies," Patrick offered.

We kept walking. They had been accosting us with some

regularity and it was my policy to say nothing unless something particularly witty occurred to me.

"Where is the old fart anyways? I guess he'll probably stay home for a while after getting his nose rubbed in it yesterday. My father says the senile old bugger had it coming." Wayne always offered his father's statements with particular relish.

Bobby spoke. "He's not senile."

"Hey guys, did you hear that? The Worm speaks."

"You don't have to listen if you don't want to."

"Pretty sharp, Wriggler. I guess if you had a thousand years to hang around with Jon-athan and Grandfather Time you might get almost normal." The remark about Grandfather Time was, in my opinion, rather good, and I tried to think of something I could do with it. Before I could come up with anything, Wayne wheeled his bike around in front of us and stopped. "Yeah, I guess hanging around with a senile old man and some sissy who likes little poems has helped you a lot."

We stepped evenly and quietly around him. All three pedalled along beside us. "It's too bad Grandpa has decided to stay away from Main Street. We all needed a good laugh. I guess that's one down Wormy. When Jon-athan goes back to wherever he came from then you'll be all alone. It'll just be you and sandcastles with a senile old man. We'll see how much of a smart ass you are then."

They then turned and rode off. We stopped and watched them go. I was angry at Wayne's calm assurance that the status quo had been restored. I thought of Helen Stadler and the many others who, to a greater or lesser extent, probably shared his view. But instead of feeling embarrassment for my grandfather, I turned to Bobby and spoke.

"I think tonight that maybe Wolfsbane and Foxglove will go up to Wayne's end of town to see what they can see. Okay Bobby?"

He nodded and smiled happily.

104

That evening, as twilight deepened, Bobby and I silently worked our way toward the back of the Maclenan's house. Skulking had become second nature to us, and following the example of Wolfsbane and Foxglove, we worked our way down the line of bushes at the edge of the schoolyard and from there into the long, untrimmed grass behind the backstop. There was no horizon behind us, not even a light-coloured building, so we were confident that we could not be seen. We were there with one of the lessons of the Western Kingdom fully in mind; careful observation will always reveal any story that might lie buried in the surroundings. In fact, we were there more as a gesture than anything else. Then, without warning, a story unfolded before us.

Wayne Maclenan stepped out on his back porch, called something back into the house and then walked straight toward us. We sank lower in the grass, but we continued to watch. Although he did not cross the backyard furtively, he did the next best thing; he was too casual. He stopped by the garden shed, not more than 30 yards from where we lay. He took his bicycle from where it leaned against the shed, and then paused elaborately, looked down at the chain and leaned the bicycle back against the shed. He crouched down and appeared to make some adjustment to the bicycle chain, but I knew it was a sham. You cannot make any adjustment to a chain by poking your forefinger at it twice. Then we saw him take a quick look toward the house and step behind the garden shed. The shed sat on concrete blocks, and he kneeled down on one knee, groped underneath it for a moment, and pulled out what looked to be a shoebox. He opened it, looked briefly inside and then from inside his shirt he took a piece of paper. He placed it in the box, and returned the box to its hiding place. He looked around briefly, but it was obvious that he thought the only risk of discovery came from the direction of the house. Finally he stepped back out from behind the shed, confidently mounted his bicycle and pedalled off.

Bobby and I raised up on our elbows and looked at each other. We were both smiling. I whispered. "Not right now, give him some time in case he forgot something."

Bobby whispered back. "Cigarettes?"

I nodded. "Or sex."

We continued to smile while we waited. Whatever it was, it was a secret, and I felt the rightness in our discovery of it. He had laughed at the Brotherhood of the Lonely Elk, and now the Brotherhood of the Lonely Elk would have its turn. After we had counted to one hundred twice, we both began to crawl toward the garden shed. We did not need to tell each other what to do. From long practice at unveiling the town's secrets we both knew. When we were shielded from the house by the garden shed, we stood up, and bent over double, ran to the shed. Bobby kept watch over the schoolyard while I groped carefully under the shed. I found the box and pulled it out. It was not a shoebox but a cookie tin. The lid came off easily, and we both crouched down and looked in. Bobby's exclamation was not up to the standards of the Western Kingdom, but it served well enough. "Jeez, look at that. And he calls us jerks."

Inside was the Mystery of Life.

To be more precise, on the top of the sheaf of papers inside the cookie tin was an advertisement ripped from a magazine. It was a picture of a woman riding on a barge. On her top half she was wearing only a brassière. The caption read, "I dreamed I sailed down the Nile in my Maidenform Bra." Beneath the top page were dozens of "Photo News of the World" pages from the *Star Weekly.* The casual observer might have thought that Wayne had an interest in agricultural oddities such as 200-pound pumpkins and prize milk cows, but both Bobby and I knew that on the "Photo News" page there would be at least one or two starlets scantily clad and smiling out at the camera from places like Hollywood or some beach in France. Beneath the "Photo News" pages was another sheaf of papers with pictures of women advertising brassières, girdles and slips. Before we had shifted through them, however, we heard a door open and a dog bark. We crouched lower and froze. We heard a car start and drive away. Bobby whispered in my ear, "See what else he's got in there. I'll go and keep watch. I'll whistle if anyone comes." Before I could say anything, he slipped around the corner of the shed, and crouching low, ran to the side of Maclenan's house.

For a moment I thought of putting the box under the shed and following him. I did not want to be left alone with Wayne's pictures. I did not know why, but they made me uneasy. The other collections we had spied out in Union had simply given me a feeling of a job well done. But Wayne's collection of pictures was different. They were tantalizing in a way I did not understand. They troubled me. I closed the box, and then I found myself sitting down and opening it up once again. I lifted the sheaf of papers out to examine them more closely.

I looked at the woman sailing down the Nile. I reasoned that she should not seem any different than any woman in a bathing-suit top, but she was. She was reclining on cushions, gazing out ahead of her. She had a very regal expression on her face, and she was clearly in the most privileged position on the barge. Part of it, I decided, was that she was in a cookie tin instead of a magazine. Part of it was also the brassière. However special her position was on the boat, her breasts seemed even more privileged, as if they were being carefully carried out in front of her rather than being a part of her.

I lifted out the "Photo News of the World" pages. Looking at all the starlets at one time, I realized for the first time that each and every one of them, regardless of what else she was doing, was leaning over toward the camera. Furthermore, each had the same expression on her face. It was a bright smile, but seeing it repeated on so many different faces made it unsettling. I held them up close to read the captions. According to the words, each of the starlets was performing some perfectly normal activity. One was writing in her journal about her experiences on a movie set, another was leaning over a birthday cake and blowing out her candles and a third was leaning over doing a new kind of calisthenic invented by the Air Force.

The women in the undergarment advertisements he had clipped out were, more or less, the same as the starlets. They stood there, bandaged up in their white brassières, girdles and slips, but all of their poses were carefully casual as if they were waiting for the bus or out shopping. Sometimes they smiled at the camera, sometimes at each other and sometimes at nothing at all. I looked up from where I had been resting the pictures on the lid of the cookie tin. I realized I had finally graduated. I was right off the end of the schoolyard, peering into a tin box filled with pictures of women. I had a strong sense of boundaries passed, but I also had an equally strong sense of how mean the graduation was; there was none of the largeness of the Western Kingdom about it, and none of the space of the roof of the Lux. And yet I knew that I wanted to continue looking through the pictures. I felt a strange kinship with Wayne, and I sorted down to the bottom of the box to where I knew, almost to a certainty, what I would find.

She was there. It was a "dirty picture," but by today's standards it was not much. She was reclining on her side, raised up toward the camera on her left elbow, she had her right arm draped down over her hips and crotch with assumed carelessness. I wondered for a moment about the secret place that was always so well-protected in the few dirty pictures I had seen. She was smiling. It was the same smile I had seen on the starlets and the women modelling undergarments. The cookie tin was filled with smiling faces. It was filled with breasts and buttocks and thighs and smiling faces, but none of the parts were connected. I tried to think of girls and women I knew reclining in such a position without their clothes on. At first the thought was ridiculous. Then I was washed with a feeling of wrongness. I folded her back up, and it occurred to me that in doing so I had made her sit up and touch her toes. I opened the paper and folded it back up again, wondering what she must be like, walking around and talking to people. I wondered what her voice sounded like. I wondered if she had friends.

I felt very young, and I suddenly wished someone would arrive, even Wayne, to tell me how to feel. I looked up at the sky to see if the first star was out, but then looked away without even bothering to search. The sky might just as well have not existed.

I heard a noise in Maclenan's backyard. In one motion I had the pictures back in the cookie tin and the cookie tin back under the shed. Bobby rose up beside me. He was out of breath, and there was great urgency in his voice.

"Jonathan."

"Is someone coming?" I looked around the corner of the shed.

"No. But what I saw..." He paused for breath. "I saw Tessa dancing. C'mon. Come and look." He started up, and I grabbed him by the shoulder.

"What do you mean you saw her. What did she say?" For no reason I could understand, I felt guilty.

"No. Listen. I didn't talk to her. I just saw her dancing. In the basement. I was finding a place to watch from and I looked in the basement window behind the rosebush. You can see through the wall."

He did not seem to be making any sense at all. I took him by the shoulder and we ran back out to the backstop. When we were once more lying in the tall grass, I told him to explain.

"It's Tessa. She's dancing down in her room in the basement. I went by to watch from the corner for anyone coming and I looked in and saw. It's beautiful, Jonathan. You can see her too. C'mon, she's probably still dancing."

"You say she's dancing in the basement, and you can see her through the wall?"

"Just her shadow. I think the wall of her room is a sheet or something, but you can see her. It's way different than when she practises at the bandstand. She takes her shirt off and it's like a story and it's better than anything I ever saw. C'mon."

"She takes her shirt off?"

"Yes. Yes, to dance better."

I looked toward the Maclenan's house. The news that Tessa was dancing in her basement without her shirt on was superimposed over the women in the cookie tin. I thought it out as I spoke.

"We can't tell anyone about this Bobby. Not even Tessa, not until I have seen it. We'll come back tomorrow night. She said lots of times that she practises every night." I looked back at the garden shed. "We have something on Wayne now, Bobby. If he bothers us, we really have something on him. Let's go back to the Lux. I want to think this out. We'll come back and watch Tessa tomorrow night."

"Jeez, I forgot all about the box."

"I'll tell you about it. We've really got him. I guarantee it. Let's go."

"Jeez Jonathan, even Wolfsbane and Foxglove couldn't do this good in just one night, could they?"

I looked over at him. "Maybe just as good, but not any better."

Back on the roof of the Lux, Bobby was purely exhilarated by the evening's adventures. I told him about the pictures in the cookie tin, concentrating mostly on the humorous image of Wayne collecting the brassière advertisements, and when I finished I told him to be sure not to tell Tessa that he had seen her dance. A ghost of complication crossed his face, but I told him it was just for a day or so until I figured everything out. He was reassured; I was not. We were lying on our backs on the roof of the Lux, looking up into the night sky, but it was the collection of parts and puzzled smiles that stayed before my eyes.

Bobby had no such problems. He rose up on one elbow and spoke to me. "Today has been about the best hasn't it Jonathan?"

"You bet."

"Jonathan?"

"Yes."

"Why do you think he had all those advertisements for underwear?"

For a moment I thought I was faced with explaining sex to him, and I did not know how to begin. "Aw Bobby, you know why he's got them."

"Sure, Mum explained that to me a long time ago, but..."

His voice sounded strange, and I rose up to look at him. He was lying on his back and shaking. I thought for a brief moment that he was crying. It was a type of waver I had never seen in him before. Then I realized he was laughing silently. He tried twice to tell me what he was laughing about. On the third attempt he was successful.

"I just thought that maybe Wayne dreams he sat behind the garden shed in his new Maidenform Bra." The nightly parade of cars were rumbling down Main Street, so no-one could hear the gasping, echoing shouts of laughter that rang up into the night sky. I laughed at the absurdity of the image. I laughed at my anxiety. I laughed at my confusion.

When the wave of laughter had rolled over us and spent itself, I stood up and walked to the edge of the roof. The town was lit up for the night. People moved below me. I knew some of their secrets, and I knew some of my own. My eyes moved away from the pools of light, and the sounds below me seemed to recede as I gazed out beyond the town to the darkened valley where I knew the river was flowing.

I realized what had happened. The Mermaid had shown up once again. This time she was not painted on the bottom of a pool. She was not even a picture lying folded and smiling on the bottom of a cookie tin. Instead, I knew she was living and breathing and dancing in a basement across town, and however mysterious she might be, she was my friend. And however forbidden it might be, I knew that the next night I would go and watch her dance.

The next day felt like the day I went to see the Castleman's mermaid. Sitting on the verandah after breakfast, I felt separate from what went on around me. I could tell my grandfather was restless and that Jennifer and my grandmother were concerned about him, but I felt removed from it and uninvolved with their worries. Bobby seemed much younger than I and foolishly happy with his world.

In the afternoon I had a similar feeling toward Tessa. She did not seem foolishly happy like Bobby, but she did seem younger. I did not feel deceitful for not telling her of the night before. Instead, I felt as if I knew more than both of them, which made me feel unfaithful to our friendship, and at the same time, protective of it.

The strongest sign of the distance I felt came in our encounter with Wayne that day. We were walking home from our afternoon by the river when he and Patrick Stadler rode up on their bicycles. As usual upon seeing us, they began to taunt us. That day Wayne chose me to start with rather than Bobby. He was, I suppose, still feeling confident from the day before. "The Brotherhood of the Lonely Jerks rides again. Watcha been doing, Jon-athan?" He turned to Patrick. "I bet he's been down at the river with his little poems. Is that it Jon-athan, have you been down by the river with your little sissy poems?" They both laughed.

From out of the distance that I felt, I heard myself speaking. "That's right. That's just what I've been doing. Anything you say."

His face darkened. He probably thought my calm, matter-of-fact tone was a new assault upon the proper order of his world.

"Yeah, well maybe I'll tell my father that you spend your

time down there with my sister. What about that, Jonathan?"

"What you say to anyone doesn't make any difference to me. I don't know why you keep bothering us. It doesn't work anymore, so why waste your time." The flat tone of my voice surprised even me.

He switched his attack. "What are you smiling about Wormy?"

I looked over at Bobby. His smile was in the process of widening. We kept walking. I hoped they would leave. Bobby's smile was dangerous.

"I asked you a question, Retard. What are you smiling about?"

Then Bobby spoke. "What's the matter Wayne, is your girdle on too tight?" It stopped all of us. I looked over in surprise. Wayne stopped his bike in complete disbelief.

"What did you say?"

"I just wondered if your girdle was on too tight."

Suddenly Wayne was in front of us. He dismounted in one smooth motion while his bike was still moving. I watched it begin a short turn, and then rattle down in the dust. Wayne's hands were clenching and unclenching. He moved toward us. Bobby and I began backing up. Off to one side, Patrick Stadler had dismounted as well, and he was shouting out, "Paste him one Wayne. Punch his lights out." Patrick's face was flushed and his voice was high and excited. Wayne's voice was very quiet.

"How would you like your teeth kicked in Bobby? Is that what you want?" Bobby continued to smile. Wayne pushed him, and he fell over backwards. When he got up he was still smiling.

"You better tell me what you're smiling about Bobby, or I'm gonna knock your teeth right down your throat."

Up on his feet again, Bobby spoke very clearly. "I just wondered if your girdle was on too tight." He gave it a two-beat pause as Wayne raised his right fist. "Or maybe you're just dreaming about sitting behind your garden shed in your new Maidenform Bra."

"What are you..." Wayne suddenly understood. With his arm pulled back to swing, he was suddenly frozen. Full comprehension seemed to take at least 30 seconds, and during that time his face went from anger, to puzzlement, to vulnerability and back to dark fury.

"You bastards. You goddamned bastards." He was still immobilized. Patrick had not understood the exchange and he was still jumping up and down in excitement and repeating, "Punch his lights out, Wayne" and "Paste him a good one".

I finally found my tongue. "That's right. You tell your father anything you like. And we'll tell anyone we like about that nifty little collection you've been making. It should be good for a laugh. I'll bet Tessa would love to know who has been ripping pages from all the magazines in the house."

The expression on his face became tinged with desperation, but he finally unfroze. He wheeled around in a half-circle and executed what I suppose was a perfect right-cross that connected with Patrick Stadler's nose. "Shut your goddamned mouth, Stadler."

Patrick sent up a howl that sounded distinctly interrogative, and Wayne spoke again. "I said shut your goddamned mouth, Snotnose." He leapt upon his bike. His jaw was clenched so that two little bumps appeared below his cheek bones. Without saying anything more, he rode off. Patrick, still completely confused and bleeding from the nose, got on his bike and followed him.

When I turned to Bobby, I thought he was in a kind of shock from the violence. "Jeez Bobby, you could have got your head knocked off."

He grabbed me by the shoulder. "Didn't you hear, Jonathan?"

"Sure I heard. We both could have got our heads knocked off."

"No, I mean what he called me Jonathan. Didn't you hear?"

"What are you talking about?"

"He called me Bobby. Not Wriggler, not Wormy, not any of the other names. He finally called me Bobby." He looked off at the retreating figures on the bicycles. He was as dazed and happy as I had ever seen him. As the importance of it sunk in, I began to smile as well.

The confrontation with Wayne was a milestone, but the events of the day were not yet over. Evening found Bobby and me once again lying in the long grass behind the backstop. Tessa was sitting on the backstep, but she could not see us. Her mother spoke to her through the screen, and Tessa stood up and went inside. We checked our signals once more. He was to whistle twice, once long and once short, if he saw anyone coming, and we would leave separately, as best we could, to meet up later on the roof of the Lux. Otherwise, I would crawl up to the corner of the house when the dance was over, and we would leave together. We reasoned that the only problem might be the unexpected appearance of Wayne, and in the midst of speculating how likely that might be, we saw the basement light come on and shine up through the backdoor screen.

I bent double and ran for the side of the house. I waited, catching my breath and listening to discover whether anyone had seen me. I saw Bobby cross the backyard toward the front, and then, as he had instructed, I knelt down and crawled between the foundation of the house and Mrs. Maclenan's rosebushes. They were well-established roses, and I wondered if Bobby had scratched his hands as badly as I was scratching mine. When I finally reached the window, I wondered if it had been even worth the trip. What I saw when I looked in seemed nothing more or less than every basement I had ever seen.

The space was dominated by a wringer washing-machine.

Exposed pipes ran down the wall, and storm windows leaned up against it. To one side there were shelves made of rough boards on which were jumbled empty containers, a few dusty jars of preserves, and two or three used cans of paint, bits of torn newspaper still sticking to their bottoms. Light came from one unshaded lightbulb suspended in the centre of the room. On the other side of the basement was a white wall which, I assumed, must be the tacked-up sheet that Bobby had spoken of, but it looked like a normal wall to me, and I wondered if Bobby had imagined the whole thing. Then I heard a voice call out.

"Tessa, please, and for the umpteenth time, shut out the basement light. How many times do I have to tell you?" I saw Tessa emerge from the door in the wall on the far side of the basement, and I instinctively ducked back from the window into the rosebushes. I held still, the need for silence making the thorns in my back and neck even sharper, fully expecting to see Tessa looking at me with a surprised expression from the basement window. She did not appear. I saw the light go out, and cautiously I looked back through the window.

The basement had changed utterly. With the light out in the main room, the light in Tessa's room made the far wall luminous. It was only a sheet after all, barred at regular intervals by the shadows of the studding. I forgot that only a moment ago it had been an ordinary basement; I did not feel the thorns that still caught me down the length of my spine; I did not remember that I had come to see the mermaid; and I did not care that spying on Tessa was, by all standards including my own, an unfair thing to do.

What I remembered—what came over me completely— was the everyday, effortless mystery of the lights dimming and the curtain rising. It commanded my attention in the same way that the Friday afternoon film commanded my attention when I sat in the unaccustomed dark of the school auditorium with the climbing ropes and volleyball nets and basketball hoops pulled up and into the shadows. It commanded my attention the way the theatre lobby of the Plaza or the Tivoli or the Towne once commanded my attention on Saturday afternoon as I stepped through the soft dark carpets and past the fishbowls and fountains that once used to grace such establishments. Suspended and in suspense, I waited for the luminous wall in front of me to magically achieve depth and dimension.

What I saw there on the screen was not some Friday afternoon film on the wonders of Greece or safety in the streets. Nor was it some Saturday afternoon epic set at the centre of the earth or twenty thousand leagues under the sea. It was not some travelling company doing *Romeo and Juliet* or *Swan Lake* or *The Nutcracker* before a fairytale-coloured backdrop; nor was it the mermaid come to life; nor the cookie tin ladies who folded and unfolded at the bottom of the box. What I saw was a story that was part myself, part Tessa and in some way, part of all that Union had been for me that summer.

The first shadow that shone through the screen was simply Tessa. I watched her silhouette as she moved about the room. She bent down and picked something up off the floor and set it on a chest of drawers or a table. Then she moved away from the wall and her shadow blurred and grew large as she crossed the room. I believe she put a record on a portable record player. Then she moved back toward the sheet wall and her shadow coalesced once more into a clear outline. She stood for a moment in profile. She pulled her hair up on the top of her head with one hand and then turned and looked back over her shoulder. Then she let go of her hair and dropped her arms to her sides. She turned back, shrugging, to face the mirror. I could almost hear her remark, "What a dope."

She pulled her sweatshirt off over her head and stepped out of her trousers. For a moment all I could see of her silhouette was the curve of breast and buttock, but before I could fix her in that image, before I could superimpose upon the wall Castleman's mermaid or the women in the cookie tin, she changed.

She took a deep, deep breath, and as she exhaled, she began to slump. In the black-and-white outline there were no details to inhibit the change. She became old. Her shoulders were tired and round. Her head was bent forward. I found myself thinking of my grandfather and how old he had been as he had retreated from Main Street. I thought of how hot the days had been. I thought of the dust. I felt a strain on my shoulders, but before I could change my position, she changed it for me.

She inhaled. Muscle group by muscle group she was reanimated as if she was breathing in something more substantial than air, until she was standing straighter than before. This time there was no chance of her being one of Wayne's pictures. Her body was too connected. Even in silhouette, the curve of her breast was part of her ribcage, which was part of her back, which was part of her shoulders and buttocks and thighs. She was so perfectly straight that for a moment I thought she was becoming Helen Stadler and that she would start turning stiffly to and fro. But then I saw who she really was; the steadfast Tin Soldier. She looked to both sides and then shouldering her rifle she began to march, and one leg or two, it made no difference to me in my happiness at recognizing her. For a moment I wanted to knock on the window and shout to her that it worked and that I had understood. Then she changed again.

Her marching steps became higher and higher in an excess of military zeal until joy in her movement intruded and the march became prancing and the soldier stopped and looked down at his feet in surprise as if they had taken on a life of their own. Her arms raised. The rifle was thrown away, and she became the cut-out ballerina whom the soldier loved. Her arms joined the dance and she pirouetted. With her arms free she took flight.

I ceased to sit back, looking through the window and the

shadow cage at her dance, and in my imagination I moved next to the black-and-white wall where she had set her imagination dancing. The images changed and flickered. The wall itself ceased to be the bars of a cage and became the tin soldier's boat with sails and mast, and her dance moved and circled like Union on a Saturday night, pitching and rolling and sailing into the darkness. The wall became the ribs of the whale that swallowed the soldier, or perhaps in the deep breathing strain of dance, became simply her rib-cage or mine. The images changed so swiftly that perhaps she became the river the soldier sailed upon. The identity of the silhouette changed from moment to moment until the dance was a current. The dust on the basement window made no difference, nor the wringer washing-machine, nor the thorns of the rose, nor the cookie tin ladies, for the dance, movement by movement, became more inevitable until it was not something that was happening outside of me but inside of me as well. She had remembered the Union that I had seen as a young child, a changeless place where the lights danced and receded in the trees of the River Hills, and I could remember Tessa's Union that was a small town far from the sea yet filled with change that broke over the streets as ceaselessly as waves. She danced other stories she could not have known. She danced over furrows that were filled with fish. She danced over beaches that were waving with wheat. She danced on the deep moss of the forest of the Western Kingdom and she danced on the roof of the Lux. She danced all over the darkness of Sortie County until I think we must have all looked up, and seeing the leaves were not turning in some breeze, wondered for a moment if the sound we heard was approaching rain.

When it was over I did not move for a long time. Then I carefully looked up past the roses and the eaves of the house; the night sky had been given back to me. It was unfathomably deep. I looked out to the front street through the roses. It was broken into a hundred separate pictures by the cross-

119

ing of the branches, and each and every one seemed unique and worthy of examination. I was smiling. The dust on the road seemed faintly green in the streetlight, and for the first time that night the smell of roses came to me. They did not smell like flowers in vases. It was not perfume. I learned for the first time that living flowers might smell differently than those that had been cut.

I did not hear Bobby whistle for me, although later he said he did so, three times in a row, and I believe him.

I did not hear George Maclenan stumble up the front walk talking to himself, although Bobby later told me about it. I think I may have started to hear him when he spoke to his wife on the back porch.

I know that I did hear Bobby's urgent, too-loud whisper, "Jonathan, Jonathan." George Maclenan heard it too.

And I did hear George Maclenan walk around the corner of the house. I saw him bend down and look straight at me through the bushes. "Sweet Jesus, what..." I saw his eyes focus farther back at the lighted wall of his daughter's room and her shadow upon that wall. "Why you little son of a..."

Bobby slapped the side of the house and called out, "Here I am."

George Maclenan stood up, looking toward Bobby. He took a few steps toward him. "Jesus, two of you little sons of..."

I rocketted up and out of the rosebush, going in the opposite direction. I sensed the pause in his movement toward Bobby. He took a confused step back toward me. The last thing I heard him say as I soared cleanly over the next door neighbour's back fence was, "Jesus Christ, the little bastards are all over."

I was running. I was running more swiftly and more effortlessly than I had ever run before. The Royals had just pulled into their driveway next door, and taking off from the small retaining wall beside the driveway, I flew straight over the hood of their car, touching down once in the exact centre, seeing the two white faces look up startled at the apparition that had just streaked by. I was still accelerating by the time I hit the schoolyard. My shirt was untucked and billowing out behind him. It was as if the dancer had taught me movement. As each foot touched the ground it seemed I could go faster. I was like a smooth flat stone, well thrown and skipping all the way across the water, seeming to gain speed every time it touches the water and leaps up again.

With some far-away part of my mind I wondered what miracle of levitation had allowed me to shoot up out of the rosebushes without being scratched to pieces. I wondered if Mr. Maclenan would catch Bobby. I wondered if he had recognized me. But mostly I was pure and simple motion, flowing swiftly through the early night of Union. Without thinking, I chose the long pathway on the east side of town, flying by the cat-tails and willow bushes. To this day I do not understand why my feet did not become wet with dew, or why the Morris' german shepherd did not bark. I awakened six blocks later in the shadows of the caragana hedge at the War Memorial. After the pure exhilaration of the run, I was struggling for breath. I also realized that as far as my breath would allow it, I was laughing.

Not more than a minute later, just as I had begun to catch my breath, a figure that could have been the shadow of myself skimmed out of the shadows beside the Hotel. I saw that Bobby, too, was going to cut through the War Memorial on his way to the roof of the Lux. I was about to step out and welcome him when I saw that George Maclenan was still in the race. With the adrenalin still pumping through me, I actually felt envious that George Maclenan had chosen to chase him and not me. Bobby was clearly winning. He was still up on the balls of his feet and racing easily across the street. George Maclenan, although he had the advantage of a longer stride and was still running fast, had begun to labour and waste his motion.

Bobby ran directly at the War Memorial where I was

standing. He came through the gap in the hedge and hurdled the strand of light chain that surrounded the enclosure. Then he performed what seemed to me in the intoxication of the moment a manoeuvre that athletically and strategically went beyond excellence. Immediately after hurdling the chain, he stopped dead, and darted into the shadow of the hedge across from me. He was Foxglove melting perfectly into his surroundings. I recognized the logic of it instantly. George Maclenan would lumber through the hedge, over the chain and then out into the darkness on the other side of the Memorial. Bobby and I would reverse our track and exit in the opposite direction. I had to clench my fists to keep from applauding, and I crouched back into the shadows and readied myself to run back out with Bobby.

Everything went perfectly right up to the chain fence. Because he was tired or because he did not have the same knowledge of Union's secret pathways as Wolfsbane and Foxglove, George Maclenan did not jump over the graceful arc of light chain. Instead, like a tired marathoner, he tried to run straight through it as if it were a finishing tape. He was unsuccessful. He was still moving at full speed, and the chain took him just above the knees; it left him lying face down in the long grass of the War Memorial. Bobby and I remained perfectly still. George Maclenan remained perfectly still as well. After a few moments he began to move. We heard a muffled, repetitive, steady stream of profanity as he rolled over on his back. It continued while he sat up. It stopped dead when he looked directly, nearly eye to eye, at Bobby.

For a moment nothing happened. Then he stood up slowly and without saying anything grabbed Bobby by the shoulder. He shook him, just once, and very hard.

"Okay mister, we are going to fix you. We are going to fix you sonny so that you don't ever sneak around anybody's daughter's window again in your entire life. Do you understand? Where is your mother? Is she working?"

Bobby made no reply.

Mr. Maclenan shook him again. "Spit it out, bucko, is she working or at home? Do you even know where she is? Good Lord, does she know where you are?"

Standing in the shadow on the other side of the Memorial, I made a discovery; I did not care that he had caught us. I stepped into the open, and spoke calmly. "His mother is at my grandparents' house. And it wasn't him who was looking. It was me."

He jumped when I spoke, and I think it was a final indignity for him. "Well, Horatio Holds the Bridge and Little Lord Fauntleroy combined in one snot-nosed kid." He stepped over to grab me by the shoulder as well. I spoke quickly, but I think it was the quietness in my voice that stopped him.

"Keep your hands off me. We can walk." I know there was no resentment in my voice. I was conscious of nothing but a calm acceptance of the fact that we had been caught.

"That's just fine with me sonny. And we'll just see how well you walk after I talk to your grandfather. If the man has any sense at all these days, you won't be walking very well tomorrow."

Although I heard what he said to us, I did not care. I did not care that he marched us past the line of people waiting for the second feature at the Lux. It was as if the dancer and the run, perhaps the whole summer, had brought me to a state of complete indifference. I knew there would be an unpleasant scene at my grandparents' house. I knew also that before the night was out the story would have circulated around the entire town. I knew, or at least I started to know, that our action would be considered a reflection not only upon Bobby and me, but upon my grandparents and Jennifer-Rose, but I did not care. In fact I think the only question that interested me even faintly as we made our solemn march down the street was whether or not my new-found indifference was to be a passing or a permanent state of mind.

When we arrived back at the verandah, the quiet light of the festive Japanese lanterns became discordant with the words that were exchanged. I did not listen closely to what was said. The words echoed around me and above me, and at times, it seemed, below me, as if I had climbed high into the grapefruit tree, and was listening to the voices floating up. I knew there were certain things that would be said whether I listened to them or not. I could hear the tones in the voices. George Maclenan was inarticulate and angry and bitter. I could hear the confusion and weariness in my grandfather's replies. I supposed that they would say all of the things that they had to say; I simply did not care.

Then George Maclenan was gone with the promise that Bobby and I would be down to apologize the next day, and then we were all standing in the bright kitchen light and Bobby was trying to explain what we had been doing. I said nothing. Perhaps I knew I could not explain the impossible series of causes and effects, the Western Kingdom, the cookie tin, Wayne and Patrick, and all the rest of the web. Grandfather's face attempted to hide his bafflement. Jennifer's face was simple with its concern and puzzlement. It was my grandmother who stopped it all short.

"Jennifer, these two boys are tired to death. We can deal with all of this in the morning. It's not going to go away, you can be sure of that." And finally all of the words and expressions were over, and I was downstairs in my bed.

It was late. Although I was very tired, I did not even think about sleep. I sat there between the lilac-scented sheets and stared at the pictures of all my aunts and uncles and cousins ranged on the bureau top and waited for the approach of guilt. My Uncle Edwin stood stiffly in front of his fighter plane somewhere in England, but the fact that he had been shot down twice over the channel failed to intimidate me. I did not care. My Aunt Janet, standing accomplished and proud in front of the Belham Normal School, her teacher's certificate in hand, had no more power to produce remorse in me than the hand-tinted photographs of Yellowstone Park and Old Faithful. Even my cousin Frederick, who was studying to be a minister, had no effect.

I did not care. I began to wonder if I had entered some new and unexpected stage of maturity where one could do something that one knew was wrong and then, to top it off, feel no remorse whatsoever. I glanced up toward the basement window. On the other side of the window, the raspberry canes were starting to grow heavy with fruit. I thought about Tessa in her basement room far across town. I wondered if she was sleeping. Then I found myself wishing fervently that I could see her come crawling behind the raspberry canes and look in at me as I had looked in at her.

It was then that care came back to me. Sitting there in bed, I realized that even if by some miracle she should appear at my window at that very moment, I would have nothing half as beautiful to show her as she had shown me.

I stood up and rummaged through the bottom drawer of the bureau. I found a stubby, worn down pencil, and in another drawer I found some old, partly used exercise books. I took them back to bed and propped up against my pillow, I leafed through them. I came upon one of my Uncle John's. I had not been looking for one of his, but it seemed right, so I turned to the back pages. They were empty.

I forgot that my aunts and uncles and cousins and Old Faithful were looking on. I ceased to smell the lilac smell of the sheets. I did not think about the raspberry canes. I did not worry that the hour grew later and later. Erasing and crossing out and beginning on a fresh page, and erasing and crossing out and beginning on another fresh page, and changing and arranging, and adding and deleting, until it seemed just right, I wrote my first poem. It was a poem for Tessa. I looked at it once and resolved to give it to her the next day in explanation for spying on her. I laid the poem to one side of the bed, and without even pausing to turn off the light, I went to sleep.

Because riddles were the only poems I really knew about, it was a riddle. Because Tessa's dance demanded no less, because the night had been what it had been, because I had found something I cared about, it was, for a first effort, not a bad poem.

Who Am I?

I move like the birds
I move like the fish
Tell stories without words
Whenever I wish
Sometimes I have one leg
Sometimes I have two
Only music is needed
To do what I do.